"How can I help you when you won't tell me anything?"

Logan's green eyes seemed to read her soul. "You've remembered more than you're telling me."

Ashley swallowed. "I *don't* remember asking for your help."

He raised an eyebrow. "You didn't seem to mind last night, when you leaped into my arms."

Of all the nerve. Her cheeks flamed instantly. "Your job, Ranger Everett, is to train me as a Big Bend ranger. Not pry into my personal life."

The clouds rolled closer, intermittently blotting out the sun, and the scent of impending rain danced in the air.

Suddenly, a sharp, deafening crack split the air, and a spray of rocks pelted the side of his face.

Too close for thunder. Too brief for a rock slide.

The crack came again, along with another burst of rocks between them, but this time he heard the telltale whizzing sound, too.

"Down!" Logan yelled, jumping toward Ashley as another bullet zinged over their heads. "Someone's shooting at us!"

Kellie VanHorn is an award-winning author of inspirational romance and romantic suspense. She has college degrees in biology and nautical archaeology, but her sense of adventure is most satisfied by a great story. When not writing, Kellie can be found homeschooling her four children, camping, baking and gardening. She lives with her family in west Michigan.

Book by Kellie VanHorn

Love Inspired Suspense

Fatal Flashback

Visit the Author Profile page at Harlequin.com.

FATAL FLASHBACK

KELLIE VANHORN

HARLEQUIN LOVE INSPIRED SUSPENSE

Recycling programs
for this product may
not exist in your area.

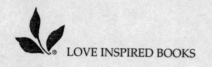

LOVE INSPIRED BOOKS

ISBN-13: 978-1-335-23254-0

Fatal Flashback

Copyright © 2019 by Kellie VanHorn

www.Harlequin.com

Printed in U.S.A.

O God, thou art my God; early will I seek thee:
my soul thirsteth for thee, my flesh longeth for thee
in a dry and thirsty land, where no water is.
–Psalms 63:1

For my family

Acknowledgments

My heartfelt gratitude goes to all who've helped
make this book possible: my fantastic critique partner,
Michelle Keener, for her thoughtful feedback;
Kerry Johnson, for her critique of the beginning;
Margie Reid, who shared her words of wisdom
on an early version.

Thanks to my wonderful editor, Dina Davis,
and the rest of the Love Inspired Suspense team
for bringing this story to life.

To my parents, Gary and Denise Parker,
and my brother Matt—thank you for letting me read
during all those family dinners.

To my husband, Jason—thank you for your boundless
encouragement. I couldn't have done it without you.
To our kids, Isaiah, Nate, Ella and Luke—thank you
for enduring long typing sessions in which
you had to get your own snacks.

Last of all, thanks to my Savior, who gifted me
with the desire to share my faith through stories.

ONE

Cold water roared through her clothes, swirling over her head and through her hair, dragging her back into consciousness. Instinctively she struggled for the surface and as soon as her head cleared the water, she coughed and gasped in a few precious breaths, wiping at her stinging eyes.

In the fading daylight the banks of the narrow river filled the horizon, impossibly high to her right but leveling out on the left. Sparse brush and skinny cottonwood trees lined the sandy river's edge.

Not a soul in sight.

Something sharp—a submerged log, maybe—jammed into her ribs. She cried out in pain but was rewarded with a mouthful of dark river water. Coughing it out, she turned against the current and kicked for the bank.

She crawled out onto the sand, tiny rocks biting into her palms, and pushed through the reeds growing at the water's edge. Collapsing onto a clear patch of ground, she struggled to catch her breath. What on earth had happened? Where was she?

The back of her head throbbed like she'd smashed it into a rock. Worse, though, was the way her brain felt like cotton fluff, disoriented and unfocused.

She squinted into the last fading rays of light, one cheek pressed down on the cool sand. As the initial blackness receded, her senses clicked slowly into place. The tall reeds stood like sentinels between her and the flat, glossy stretch of dark river water, barely visible in the dying sunlight. She shivered as a light breeze drifted over her drenched clothes.

Sitting up slowly, she pressed a hand to the throbbing place on the back of her head. When she pulled it away, a red, sticky film coated her fingers.

Her heart jumped in her chest. If only this horrible groggy feeling would go away, she could figure out where she was. What to do now.

Some distance to her right, the river disappeared into a deep canyon with jagged cliff walls rising on both sides. From the way the current ran, she must've fallen in back there, before the cliffs became impassably steep.

That way was west—the last bit of sun was still visible dipping down behind the rim of the canyon, sending streaks of pink and orange through the distant clouds.

In the other direction, to the east, the landscape flattened out and groves of cottonwood trees grew along the riverbank. No sign of civilization for as far as she could see.

How did she end up here, in the middle of nowhere?

"Ashley," she said softly, more to reassure herself than anything else. "My name is Ashley. Thompson?"

She rolled the last name around on her tongue. Sounded right.

Somewhere through the haze in her brain, she remembered that something terrible had happened—something related to why she was here, wherever *here* was. But she couldn't remember for the life of her what it was—only that it hurt, so badly her stomach clenched into a tight, aching knot.

She pressed her hands to her temples, her forehead, her eyes, trying to calm her pounding heart. Panicking wouldn't solve anything or help her remember.

Something hard dug into her hip as she sat with her legs to one side. Fumbling in her pocket, her hand closed around the smooth, cold and heavy object, then dropped it onto the sand.

A gun.

She slid backward, staring at the dark weapon lying there like a rattlesnake ready to bite.

Law enforcement. That had to be it. She stared down at her clothing, as if her soggy black pants and white blouse could explain everything. Even though it'd been in her pocket, she had a holster. The gun had to be hers. Legally, she hoped.

And the clothes seemed familiar enough. At least they fit. She struggled to remember anything—her last meal or her last ride in a car or her last day at work—but there was nothing. Just a vast, blank space in her mind, as if someone had siphoned away her entire identity beyond her first name. How was it possible she had no idea where she was or how she had gotten there?

And what on earth was she supposed to do now?

Her lips parted to utter a prayer, but she checked herself almost instantly because, along with that certainty about her name and the sense that something terrible had happened, came the knowledge she wasn't on speaking terms with God.

She shivered. Night was coming and she had no idea where to go. The thought of wandering around looking for help in the dark was horribly unappealing.

She crawled back toward the gun and picked it up,

tentatively at first, but as her hand closed around it, a familiar sense of security washed over her. She clung to that tiny bit of comfort and clasped her knees to her chest, staring out across the desert. Hoping against reason that help would come.

Logan Everett walked across the parking lot to his Jeep. The meeting with the river ranger and the border patrol agents had taken longer than he'd expected, and the sun had begun its final descent behind the Mesa de Anguila to the west.

He could still get in a good chunk of the drive back to Panther Junction before the onset of total darkness, but he had a nagging feeling something was wrong.

That black sedan that had turned around in front of the general store—he had seen it from the window during their meeting—had headed down toward Santa Elena Canyon a good hour ago, and it hadn't returned. Granted, it was hard to tell from his vantage point inside the Castolon ranger office, but it had looked like the driver, a woman, was alone.

Now that it was almost dark, she shouldn't still be there. She couldn't drive that sedan on the dirt road up to Big Bend National Park's west entrance at Terlingua and, as far as pavement went, the canyon was the end of the line.

Logan exhaled a long breath that matched his never-ending day. Well, it wouldn't hurt to check. He had learned that the hard way. He trusted his instincts—they hadn't failed him yet—and if it turned out she was fine, or not there anymore, at least he'd be able to sleep tonight knowing he'd made sure.

An image flashed into his mind—a man's body in a

ranger uniform, half a mile off the trail. Vultures circling above in the 110-degree heat. More than circling.

Logan shuddered. No, he was not going to think about Sam. Not now.

Please, Lord, he prayed, *keep this woman safe*.

The Santa Elena Canyon parking lot lay in deep shadow by the time he pulled in. The lot was empty except for the black car, its driver conspicuously absent. Logan parked and got out, pulling a flashlight from the Jeep's glove compartment.

He walked toward the trailhead, scanning his light across the sand for footprints. There were plenty, since the canyon trail was one of the most popular in the park. He frowned. It was also short enough that the woman should have returned by now.

He stopped when the arcing sweep of his light caught a set of footprints off to one side, leading toward the river. Annoying hikers. It was like they couldn't read the signs plastered all over the place.

Stay on the trails. Not only did it preserve the environment, there were enough ways to get injured without needing to wander off looking for more trouble.

Picking his way carefully, Logan followed the tracks until they ended at the river. Here the sand was wet and the marks were much clearer. Too large for a woman. The same single pair of tracks circled back to the parking lot.

Nothing. As he turned to leave, his flashlight glinted off something lying in the brush a short distance downstream.

He snatched it off the damp sand. A woman's silver wristwatch. His breath caught in his chest. Judging by its near flawless condition, it hadn't been there long.

Hastening his pace, he walked downstream along the bank, sweeping the light ahead. He hadn't gone far when he froze. Movement—there, to the left. A woman. And she was clearly alive, because she was lying on her stomach, arms out in front of her, pointing a handgun at his chest.

He slowly lifted both hands, the law-enforcement side of him sizing her up within seconds—midtwenties, maybe five feet, eight inches in height, thin yet muscular build. She had the same long, dark hair of the driver he had seen earlier.

Only now it was wet and hung in clumps around her pale face and her sandy, soaked shirt clung to her shoulders and arms.

"Whoa, it's okay. I'm here to help you. You don't need the gun." He angled the flashlight to one side and inched toward her, hands up. "Put the gun down, okay? There's no reason for anyone to get hurt."

"Who are you?" Her voice was high-pitched and trembling.

"Logan Everett. I'm a law-enforcement ranger." He pointed at the brown arrowhead badge on his shirt. "National Park Service."

The woman sat up, keeping the gun steady. Clearly she was no stranger to handling weapons.

Law enforcement?

Or criminal? Crime was rare in Big Bend, but it *did* happen.

"Don't come any closer." Her brown eyes grew wide, the whites glistening in the fading light.

Logan stopped, crouching down ten feet away from her and holding the silver wristwatch out for her to inspect. "Is this your watch?"

"I...I don't know," she stammered. "Stay back."

There was a definite edge of panic in her voice. Something had happened to her and she was still terrified.

"Hey—" he reached toward her "—we're on the same side. How did you get out here?" The wary, frightened look in her large, dark eyes reminded him of a cornered animal.

Her forehead wrinkled and her eyes slipped out of focus as she shook her head. "I…I fell into the river."

He nodded reassuringly, even as he tried to calculate how she could have fallen in. He couldn't see her feet clearly from his present position, but he didn't think it was likely the tracks by the river had been hers. Odd.

When she didn't say anything else, he asked, "From the trail?"

"I…" She bit her lip, brows furrowed, and lowered the gun slightly. He straightened and inched forward, taking advantage of her distraction. "I don't remember."

Her eyes were still out of focus and her hands shook as she held the gun.

"Are you injured?"

She took one hand off the gun, reaching for the back of her head. When she pulled her hand away, red smeared her fingertips. She stared at the blood, the gun drooping in her other hand.

That explained it—well, at least her obvious confusion. Poor woman. She probably had a concussion.

He stepped forward, holding his hands up, inching closer and closer. Like approaching an injured mountain lion, only without the tranquilizer darts.

When he was a few feet away he dropped down onto his knees. He was directly in front of her by the time she looked at him again and, before she could react, Logan had the gun out of her hand and safely tucked into his waistband.

The woman stared at him, her expression torn between fear and confusion.

"There." He offered her a grin. "Now that you're not going to kill me, maybe I can help you."

He peered at the back of her head. Her long, brown hair was matted into a knot by the blood and there was a large bump. Had she fallen? Or was it foul play?

"Where am I?" She turned wide, dark eyes up to him.

"You must've taken quite a blow to the head. This is Big Bend National Park, in west Texas. And we're right outside Santa Elena Canyon on the Rio Grande."

"Texas?"

"Yes, ma'am."

She winced as she pulled back onto her knees.

"Easy." Logan held out his hand. She glanced up at him warily. "You might have other injuries."

She rubbed a hand slowly over her lower ribs. "I hit something in the water," she mumbled.

"We need to get you checked out. Do you think you can walk?"

When she nodded, he gently helped her to her feet. She swayed unsteadily for a moment, clinging to his arm.

"Do you remember your name?" He picked a path for them around the low brush back toward the trailhead parking lot.

"Ashley." She gripped his arm a little tighter as she stumbled over something in the growing darkness, and Logan swung his light to the ground. Despite her little dunk in the Rio Grande, a light scent of something sweet, like berries, emanated from her hair.

"What's the last thing you remember, Ashley?"

"I…I remember…" She grew thoughtful for a moment, chewing on her lip. When she spoke again, her voice held a note of hope. "Taking a cab. Yes, that was it."

"I think we can rule out that being today. So, you have no idea why you're here in Big Bend?"

She shook her head but a brief flicker of some emotion passed over her face. Grief? Or anger? He wasn't sure, but clearly something lurked under the surface and she didn't want to share or couldn't remember.

Either way, pretty women dressed in tailored slacks didn't turn up in the Rio Grande for no reason.

When they reached the parking lot, Ashley stared blankly at the two vehicles in the lot—the rental car Logan suspected was hers and his NPS Jeep.

"Recognize it?"

She dug into one of her pockets. "No. But I do have a set of keys that survived the river. I may as well try them."

The river had wrecked the electric key fob, but she was able to open the driver's door using the key. As she searched the interior for personal items, he called in the plates to a park dispatcher.

A quick search confirmed it was a rental, from an Enterprise in El Paso, Texas—she must've flown in to the airport there.

"The name?" he asked the dispatcher.

The radio crackled. "Watson. Ashley Watson."

Ashley climbed back out of the car, holding the black blazer that completed her suit—absolutely the wrong clothing for the desert—as well as a small handbag.

"Ms. Watson?" Logan gestured at the purse. "Did you find some identification?"

She frowned, rubbing her forehead with a knuckle as she stared at the closed purse.

"Everything okay?"

"Sure." Her expression cleared but the air of confusion still lingered—must be from the head injury. She fumbled with the purse's zipper and dug out a wallet, staring at the driver's license inside for a long moment before handing it to him. Her forehead creased again.

Logan took the license from her clammy fingers. *Ashley Watson*. Issued in the District of Columbia. His brows pulled together. "No idea what brings you to Texas, Ms. Watson? You're a long way from home."

She leaned against the car. Her face was pale but she held his gaze. "No, but it'll come back to me. Otherwise, I know where to go home. Now, if you want to point me in the right direction to a medical facility, I can drive myself. I'm sure you have other places to be."

Was she trying to get rid of him? Did she remember more than she was letting on?

"Really?" He raised an eyebrow. "You think I'd let you drive in your condition?"

"I'm feeling better. Besides—" she nodded toward his Jeep "—you probably have a cold pack in there for my head, right?"

"For starters, the road to the nearest medical facility is that way." He pointed across the parking lot toward a nearly invisible dirt road leading into the desert to the north. "And second, you'll be coming with me to park headquarters in Panther Junction after we go to the clinic."

"Why?" Somehow she managed to look both helplessly lost and irritated at the same time.

"Because it's illegal to carry a firearm in this park without a permit unless you're in law enforcement."

"So, what? You're going to arrest me after I almost drowned?" Sparks flared in her brown eyes.

"No." Logan sucked in a slow breath, searching for the tattered shreds of his patience. "I'm going to bring you in for questioning. Unless you've got a Texas-approved license to carry somewhere in there, too."

She inhaled sharply, eyes widening. *Nervous?* But why? "I'm sure there's a good reason for the gun." She dug inside her blazer pocket, her brow furrowing when her fingers came away empty. "I have a holster."

"Maybe. But we'll let the chief ranger decide."

She closed and locked her car door and then took the arm he offered, cold fingers clutching his elbow, and he escorted her to the Jeep.

He helped her into the passenger seat and handed her a thick gauze pad from a first-aid kit. "Press this to the wound, and here's an ice pack for the swelling."

Ashley took the gauze, wincing as she touched it to the injury. A wave of pity washed through him. The ride to Terlingua over that washboard dirt road was going to hurt.

She sat silently in the passenger seat, a hand pressed to her eyes, as he did his best to steer around the lumpiest sections of the road.

They'd been driving for maybe thirty minutes when headlights appeared in the rearview mirror, two tiny orbs bouncing in the distance.

Ashley craned her head over her shoulder. "Somebody else uses this road?"

"Yeah…once in a while." He frowned. The lights were growing bigger much faster than they should be. Usually only Terlingua locals and lost tourists used this road, and neither was foolish enough to go that fast.

Only a few minutes passed before the other vehicle was nearly on their tail, its headlights glaring off the dashboard and mirrors so brightly he had to squint. A truck, judging by the height of the lights.

Better to let them pass than get into an accident out here. He slowed the Jeep, driving closer to the side to allow the truck space to pass. "Impatient driver. Going to break an axle at this rate."

Impatient *and* reckless—couldn't they see this was an NPS vehicle? He'd be sure to get the plate number and call it in.

But the truck didn't pass. Instead it veered to the right with them and accelerated.

"What...?" Logan muttered. "Hold on!"

The driver was going to ram them.

TWO

Ashley scrabbled to find the handle inside the door as Logan jerked the steering wheel to the left. The Jeep swerved, its tires slipping on the loose dirt. Behind them, the truck eased off the gas long enough to follow them into the center of the road.

Could it be whoever had attacked her at the river coming back to finish the job? She shivered, clutching the door handle hard enough her fingers hurt.

The truck shot forward again, bumping the rear of the Jeep as Logan accelerated. Not hard enough to release the air bags, but enough to whip her forward and lock her seat belt. She grimaced as her head smacked back into the seat.

Logan's jaw clenched as he cranked the steering wheel to the left, trying to move the Jeep out of the way. He yanked a handheld radio out from its holder and tossed it onto her lap. "Call the dispatcher."

She fumbled for the call button, holding the radio to her mouth, but it slipped out of her fingers as the Jeep jostled and bounced over the rough edge of the road.

"Hold on," Logan said again as he slammed down the gas pedal.

Headlights filled the cabin as the truck pummeled

into their bumper again. Logan grunted as he struggled to keep control of the steering wheel and Ashley clung to her seat as the Jeep careened toward cactuses and brush growing on the side of the road.

They rolled to a stop in a sea of prickly pears and spiky grasses. She let out a little sigh of relief as the truck swerved past them.

Until it stopped fifty feet ahead. Both doors opened. Whoever was getting out wasn't coming to lend them a hand.

Logan gestured at the Jeep's floorboard as he drew his gun. "Get down."

She swallowed, sliding a hand toward her seat belt to unbuckle it, but at that moment more headlights appeared in the distance. This time, from the opposite direction.

Ahead of them, the truck's doors slammed shut and its engine roared back to life. A second later it barreled away toward Terlingua in a cloud of dirt stained red by its taillights.

Logan flipped on the interior cab light. "You okay?" His brows pulled together in concern.

She took a couple of deep breaths, trying to slow her pounding heart, and nodded. "But I didn't get the plates." She retrieved the radio from her feet and handed it to him.

"It's okay," he said after calling in the incident. "Still a few miles to Terlingua. Maybe local police can get there in time."

He coaxed the Jeep out of the loose sand and back onto the packed road. When they passed the oncoming car a few minutes later, Logan flagged down the driver, but the man, a Terlingua resident, hadn't caught the truck's plates, either.

The vast Texas sky was full of stars by the time they

reached the medical clinic. Ashley's head was swimming. A memory had come back as they'd jostled along on the road—the bumps had reminded her of tractor rides and apple-picking with her parents and brother. More childhood memories had seeped in after that one, filling her with relief.

Then that truck had showed up to ram them.

After what had just happened, it was a good thing Logan wanted to take her back to park headquarters. Plus, she hadn't found anything in her car other than a suit jacket and her purse. Big Bend National Park was remote—it seemed unlikely she would travel all the way out here without any luggage. But where was she staying?

And, more pressing, who was after her?

After a nurse took her to a private room, she rummaged through her handbag to see what else it contained besides the wallet. There wasn't much. A tube of lipstick. Hand sanitizer. A couple of pens. She pulled out the wallet and stared at the driver's license.

Washington, DC. Was that where she lived? The city name felt right. Comfortable.

But the license hadn't been issued to Ashley Thompson... Why? Were all her hunches and instincts wrong? She shivered, tucking the license back into its slot and pulling out the piece of paper sticking out of the next one.

A photograph.

She stared for several long minutes at the picture. It was a man, maybe college-aged, with short, dark hair and hazel eyes. A relative? Maybe her brother? The photo was well worn around the edges, as if she had handled it and carried it with her for some time.

Why did looking at him make her stomach clench into a tight knot?

Logan was pacing back and forth in the lobby when

the clinic's only doctor escorted her back out. The ranger's dark green eyes locked onto her as she stepped into the room, and Ashley's breath unaccountably hitched. She hadn't seen him clearly before, what with the setting sun and her throbbing head, but in this lighting, it was obvious the man was in his element as a park ranger. Clean-shaven, tanned, sandy-brown hair. Just over six feet tall, she guessed, and at peak fitness. Every movement came with easy confidence.

She turned away from his speculative gaze. Maybe he didn't believe her about the memory loss. Maybe he thought she was trying to cover something up.

Thankfully he turned to the doctor, giving Ashley the chance to get her thoughts back under better regulation before she had to speak.

"How is she?" Logan asked.

"Her skull's intact and the wound itself should heal up nicely. Based on the symptoms she's described, I'd say she's sustained a level two, possibly level three, concussion. The good news is the CT scan is clean—no internal hemorrhaging. She needs to take it easy for several days until her symptoms are gone, and more specifically, she'll need to be monitored closely for the next twenty-four hours."

Several days? Ashley resisted the urge to frown. She had no idea why she was in Texas—how, exactly, was she supposed to lie around and relax?

Logan nodded, eyeing her thoughtfully. "And her memory loss?"

"Retrograde amnesia—limited to events prior to the injury. But given her lucidity now and her other test results, I'd say the prognosis for a full recovery is good. I expect she'll start getting her memories back anytime now, the older ones first. Childhood through adolescence typically come back first, followed by more recent events. You may be able to help the recovery with exposure to memory triggers. But," he said to Ashley, "whatever happened right before the trauma might not come back at all if your brain lost it from short-term memory."

She nodded. "Well, hopefully that won't be the case. I'd like to know what happened to me."

"Of course. At least you've found yourself in good hands with Ranger Everett."

Ashley thanked him and followed Logan outside, hoping he hadn't noticed the heat creeping into her cheeks at the doctor's comment. Especially since he couldn't be the only attractive man she'd ever been around in her life.

"How are you feeling?" he asked.

She climbed up into the passenger seat, avoiding the hand he offered. "Better. My head isn't pounding anymore and things aren't quite so fuzzy."

"Do you remember anything about coming to Big Bend?"

She shook her head. "It's like there's a blank spot in my mind and, beyond that, a lot of vague impressions rather than certainties."

"That's to be expected, I guess." He steered the Jeep toward the main road into the park. "It'll take us an hour to get back to Panther Junction. Try to get some rest and we'll find a place for you to sleep once we're finished."

Sleep seemed out of the question, but Ashley was glad for an excuse to stop talking. He hadn't asked her any more personal questions, but she could almost hear them on the tip of his tongue. *What else did you find in the purse? Why did you come to Texas? What secrets are you keeping?*

Thinking about it made her brain hurt. Logan hadn't said anything more about what had happened to her, either, but given the incident with the truck, it seemed obvious someone was after her. Probably the same someone who had hit her in the head. But who? And why? There had to be some reason she was carrying a gun. Hopefully her memories would come back before whoever it was returned to finish the job.

Ashley was out cold by the time Logan pulled into park headquarters in Panther Junction. She didn't even stir as he turned off the engine. He sat watching her for a moment under one of the few motion-activated lights in the parking lot.

Something about her seemed familiar... Maybe her mannerisms. Or the shape of her eyes. Or the way she spoke. He couldn't quite put his finger on it, or how he could possibly have met her before.

How had she ended up in the Rio Grande Wild and Scenic River? Wearing a business suit, no less. She had been barefoot all night, so he could only guess she'd lost her shoes in the river. Judging by the outfit, he assumed they would have been heels, the worst possible choice for a trip to the desert.

And the gun. Why the gun? The way Ashley had pulled it out and trained it on him was evidence enough she knew about weapons. Those actions came from physical memory, created by years of experience.

What worried him most was that incident with the truck. Her head injury and the fall into the river *could* have been an accident. The unidentified set of tracks along the river's edge might have been coincidence. But the truck? No doubts there. The driver had intended to run them off the road. If that other vehicle hadn't scared them off, he hated to think what might've happened. And since Terlingua police hadn't been able to find anything, there were no suspects to question.

What kind of trouble was Ashley in?

Even though Big Bend shared several hundred miles of border with Mexico, its vast, empty deserts and rugged mountains prevented far more criminal activity than the rangers could. More visitors got into trouble from dehydration than anything else. In fact, Logan couldn't even remember the last attempted homicide.

He frowned. The answers appeared to be locked away in that woman's mind, inaccessible. Maybe the chief ranger and the park superintendent would have better success.

"Ashley—" he nudged her shoulder "—we're here."

She sat up, rubbing her eyes, and then stumbled blearily beside him to the park office, waiting as he unlocked the door. By now it was after ten o'clock at night and the place was dark and empty inside. Logan flipped on a light and left Ashley in a chair near the receptionist's desk while he telephoned Chief Ranger Ed Chambers and Superintendent Dick Barclay.

Housing for the staff assigned to Panther Junction was a short walk from headquarters, so they only waited a few minutes before the others arrived.

Ed Chambers stepped in first. Tall, with graying hair and a face lined from years working outside, the chief looked like a quintessential career ranger. And he was exceptionally good at what he did—Logan could only hope that one day his career record would be half as accomplished as Ed's. Until then, he was grateful to have his mentorship, friendship and guidance.

The superintendent, on the other hand, stuck out like a sore thumb. He had only been stationed at Big Bend for the past six months and Logan expected him to throw in the towel any day now. But Dr. Barclay—as he insisted on being called—still kept showing up every day to make Logan's life a little more difficult.

"Dr. Barclay. Ed," Logan greeted them. "Here's the woman I told you about."

To Logan's surprise the superintendent strode over to Ashley and extended his hand. "Ms. Watson, I'm so sorry to hear you were involved in an accident."

Ashley blinked up at him like a pale-faced snowy owl. "You…you've met me?" she stammered.

Barclay turned surprised eyes on Logan, as if all the confusion was his fault. "Excuse us, Ms. Watson. We'll be right back."

Logan and Ed followed him across the room, where the superintendent dropped his voice to a whisper. "Everett, what happened to her?"

He shrugged. "Head trauma, concussion, memory loss. We're not sure of the full extent." He went on to explain how he had found her beside the river. "I brought her here because she was armed without a permit. And obviously I couldn't drop her off at a motel somewhere."

Ed clapped him on the shoulder, a glint in his eyes. "You did the right thing, bringing her here."

Logan couldn't shake the feeling that Ed was laughing at his expense. He pressed his lips together, waiting for the punchline. "What? What is it?"

"She's a new ranger, Everett," Barclay snapped. "She arrived from El Paso this afternoon."

"A new r-ranger?" he spluttered. "Why didn't anyone tell me?"

"Unique case. This hire didn't go through the normal channels—ordered by someone at the Department of the Interior. You don't need to know all the details."

"So, what about the gun?" He looked from Ed to Barclay. "No permit. She wasn't in uniform—"

"It's not important." Barclay cut him off with a shake of his head. He held out his hand expectantly toward Logan, who pulled Ashley's gun from his belt and gave it to the superintendent. "I'll talk to her about it. Everett, see to it she gets some rest and, when she's recovered, you can begin her training."

A pit opened in his stomach. "But surely I'm not the right one for that job. What about Rogers or Evanston?"

"You're the only one for the job right now, because you're the one she knows. Now quit arguing."

"Of course, sir." He bit his tongue as the superintendent walked back to Ashley.

Why him? He turned to Ed for help. Of all people, Ed knew what he'd gone through. How he wasn't ready to train anyone yet, not after the way he had failed the last ranger he'd trained. It had only been three months.

And Sam Thompson had been a natural outdoorsman in top physical condition. He had absorbed everything Logan had taught him like a sponge taking in water. Or so Logan had thought until the day the search-and-rescue team had found what was left of Sam's body baking in the June sun, a half mile off the Dodson Trail. Cause of death?

Dehydration.

So much for being a good instructor.

The worst part? That place in his gut, where intuition lived, had told him something wasn't right, that Sam was taking too long on his patrol. It was Sam's first time on the high Chisos trails alone, and Logan had almost called in a search team that afternoon when it grew late.

But he had talked himself out of it. *Sam is a good*

ranger. He can take care of himself. He'll be back any-
time now.

By the time the SAR team was mobilized the next
day, it was too late.

Somehow, Sam had gotten lost and ended up down
Juniper Canyon and onto the Outer Rim in the open
desert. Death by dehydration had probably come within
a matter of hours. The fine line between life and death
was even thinner when summer arrived in the desert.

Ed clapped him on the shoulder in his annoyingly
brisk and cheerful way. "It's time to get back out there,
Logan. You're good at this job and you've been blaming
yourself way too long. Sam's death wasn't your fault."

"Ed…" He ran a hand through his hair. "If I couldn't
keep him alive, with all his experience, how am I going
to protect *her*?" He gestured to Ashley, her disheveled
business suit glaringly out of place in the bright lights
of headquarters.

"Protect her?" Ed's brows pinched together. "She's a
law-enforcement ranger. You don't have to protect her."

Wrong word. Why had he said that? Probably because
she looked so vulnerable, helpless even, sitting over there
talking to the superintendent.

"I'm sorry, I didn't mean 'protect.' Of course she can
take care of herself. I meant… It's the desert here and…"
His voice trailed away as he struggled to decide exactly
what he did mean.

"It's okay, Logan. I think I understand." Ed's expression was far too perceptive.

"Stop looking at me like that." Logan tugged at his
suddenly uncomfortable shirt collar. "Whatever you're
thinking, it isn't true."

"I'm thinking you'd better show her to her quarters.

And I'm thinking maybe you're finally ready to forget Erin Doyle."

"I let her go a long time ago."

Ed's smirk showed he wasn't convinced. "Right." He clapped Logan on the shoulder again. "Let me know if you need anything."

THREE

Ashley's head clouded over again as she waited for Logan to finish talking to the chief ranger. She wanted to get into bed, sleep for the next fifty years and wake up when everything was back to normal. Whatever "normal" was.

Ms. Watson, the superintendent had called her. It matched her driver's license, but not that vague impression she'd had earlier that her last name was Thompson. Was she keeping her real last name a secret for some reason?

But how on earth did she get a job here as a ranger without her real name? And why would she even want to work here in the first place? She couldn't remember any details about her old job, or *life* for that matter, but she was pretty sure it didn't have anything to do with roughing it out in the desert.

She rubbed absently at one of her arms, realizing her sleeve was still full of sand. Her clothes were dry now, but her hair was a tangled mess and nothing sounded better than a hot shower and a bed.

Logan glanced at her from across the room, his expression a mixture of confusion and concern. Finally the chief ranger clapped him on the shoulder and the flicker of emotion was replaced by a smile as he approached.

"I guess I should call you Ranger Watson now."

"Apparently so." She ignored the way her stomach curdled. The whole thing felt like a lie and she hated hiding the truth, whatever the truth was. Especially when she had no idea why. But the superintendent had asked to talk to her when she was ready to return to duty. Maybe he had some answers. "It's okay if you want to keep calling me Ashley instead."

He smiled. "Ashley, it is. And please call me Logan. Only people who don't like me use my last name."

"I doubt there's anyone who doesn't like you." She would have to add warm, considerate and easygoing to her mental description of him.

"You might be surprised." He held out his hand to help her up. "Come on, I'll walk you home."

She hesitated for a fraction of a second but, deciding it would be better not to embarrass him, took his hand. The sudden warmth of his skin on hers sent an electric jolt through her stomach and she swayed ever so slightly.

"Steady?" He still held her hand.

Her cheeks burned. "Yes." She pulled away the second he let go.

"Sure you don't want to take my arm?"

She swallowed. "No, thank you. I'll be fine." She had to be fine, because she wasn't going to let herself keep clinging to him, not when he affected her so unreasonably.

Logan opened the door and she followed him out into the dark, starlit night. They walked around to the back of the building and along a path toward a cluster of homes.

"It's all government housing," Logan said. "I'm sure you've heard all this before, but residence in the park is mandatory for rangers. Apparently you already checked in at Panther Junction earlier today and you were given a housing assignment."

Something Ashley had no recollection of… Yet another memory lost in the black swirl of her mind. To fend off the panic, she asked, "Do all the rangers live here?"

"No. There are residences at Castolon and Rio Grande Village, too, down by the river."

She followed him into a section of single homes at the west end of the complex. The Chisos Mountains loomed like jagged black teeth over the rooftops. Warm light issued from a few of the houses they passed, but the rest of the street was dark. "Aren't there any streetlights?"

"No. The park is trying to eliminate light pollution, and this street is being renovated." He waved at the dark houses beyond hers. "Those are mostly empty—that's why they're so dark."

"Sounds cozy."

"Don't worry, you'll get neighbors soon enough."

She fished the key ring out of her pocket, happy to find she had a key that turned in the lock. Finding the light switch inside the door, she flipped it and stepped over the threshold. Nothing looked familiar, but at least the collection of luggage was promising. Maybe she'd find some clues as to why she was there.

"Recognize anything?" Logan leaned against the inside of the door frame, arms folded casually across his chest, watching her with those pensive green eyes.

She shook her head.

"Well, I'll leave you to get settled. You should have some groceries in the fridge, compliments of Sandy, the receptionist. Sure you don't need anything else right now?"

"No."

"Then I'll be back to check on you in an hour. Doctor's orders."

She grimaced. "Guess sleep isn't on the schedule for tonight."

"Not with a head injury." His lips curved into a crooked smile.

He turned to leave, but Ashley called after him. "Logan?"

"Yeah?"

"Thank you." Her toes curled in embarrassment. Apparently being rescued wasn't a typical experience. "For helping me tonight."

He grinned. The light from the front porch danced in his eyes. "It was my pleasure."

Logan walked down the dark street toward his own home, trying to quell the smile that kept popping onto his face.

Business. This was all about business. Part of his job was helping anyone in distress, and just because that someone was living in Panther Junction, and he had to train her, was no reason to keep thinking about her. Beyond having to check on her every hour, of course—doctor's orders.

In fact, their work relationship was an excellent reason *not* to think about her, whatever Ed Chambers might say to the contrary. Seven years out here had taught him a number of painful lessons and one of them was never to fall for a fellow ranger. Because sooner or later they all left when they got the chance.

He could almost hear Erin's voice ringing in his head, as if she were still standing there arguing with him, even after all these years. She had been so beautiful, with her blond hair and green eyes a few shades lighter than his own. *A perfect match*, his family had said.

But she had hated living in Big Bend. Eight hundred thousand acres of desert, mountains and river—some of the most beautiful, remote country in the lower 48— and she had *hated* it. The place he never wanted to leave, because it had gotten into his blood, into his very soul.

He'd been ready to propose, sure that Erin was the one and convinced she would stay here for his sake— no, for their sake, at least until they could talk about asking for a reassignment. But love wasn't enough. *He* wasn't enough.

She had left, without ever looking back.

That was five years ago and no woman had caught his attention since. Probably a self-defense mechanism. Apparently it had decided to fail today. That was both unfortunate and unacceptable, because something about Ashley—maybe it was the suit, or her pale skin, or the fact she had no idea why she was here—screamed, *I don't belong in the desert.*

Keeping her alive until she could be reassigned was going to be enough trouble. He didn't need to add personal feelings. And the last thing he wanted, after the long years waiting for God to heal his broken heart after Erin, was to risk anything like it again. No, the newest ranger would be his trainee and his colleague, and nothing more.

He returned dutifully to her house an hour later, glad to find her condition appeared stable. Pupils weren't abnormally dilated, responses all coherent. Four repeat visits over the course of the night showed similar promise of no regression. She greeted him with a groggy smile each time before stumbling back to the sofa where she'd decided to crash for the night. By 7:00 a.m. he advised her to go to sleep in her bed. He'd come back and check on her later in the day, after getting some work done in the office.

He nearly collided with someone on his way into head-quarters. Will Sykes, one of the newer rangers, who had started just prior to Sam Thompson. "Will, a little distracted this morning?"

"What?" The dark-haired younger man glanced up, his thoughts obviously elsewhere. He was probably heading out to one of the campgrounds on patrol. "Oh, sorry. I guess so."

Logan moved aside to let him out the door, but Will stopped, lowering his voice enough that Sandy Barnes at her receptionist desk wouldn't overhear. "Hey, I heard you pulled somebody out of the Rio Grande last night. What happened?"

Word certainly got around fast in this park. "Actually, I found her on the riverbank. We're not sure how it happened."

"Good thing you showed up." His Adam's apple bobbed and he tapped his thumb against his clipboard. "Was she all right?"

"Bit of memory loss, but she'll be okay. You'll meet her soon—turns out she's the newest ranger." Logan glanced at his watch. Only fifteen minutes until his first meeting of the day. "Listen, Sykes, I—"

The clipboard clattered to the ground and Will stooped to retrieve it.

"—need to get going."

"Of course." Will's face had gone uncharacteristically pale.

Must be thinking about Sam, too. They'd been friends and Sam's death had affected Will almost as much as Logan. Ashley was their first new law-enforcement ranger since the accident. It wasn't a surprise Will would be shaken up.

Logan squeezed the younger man's shoulder, trying to mimic Ed's natural gift of encouragement. "Nobody can replace him, but it'll be good to have someone new on the team."

"Yeah." Will left through the front door, waving on his way out.

A file for Ashley Watson lay on Logan's desk, as Ed had promised. It didn't contain anything exceptional. Twenty-seven years old, hometown of New Haven, Connecticut—that might explain why picturing her in the desert seemed like such a stretch. She had passed NPS training school with flying colors. Before going into law enforcement, she had worked for the Department of the Interior in Washington, DC—a desk job—but maybe those connections had got her the position out here.

Nothing to explain why she'd been down at the canyon yesterday, in a suit, with a gun. A gun she handled so well it looked like years of instinct, he might add—not just six months of park service training.

No word had come back on the truck, either. Whoever had attacked them had managed to vanish into the desert. Barclay had looked concerned but could only tell him to file a report. What else could they do? Nobody could explain how the newest ranger had become a target in a park where violent attacks by anything other than mountain lions were almost unheard of.

Maybe Logan would have to make his afternoon visit to her a bit longer, see if he could ask any questions that might jog her memory. Purely for the sake of investigation, of course.

* * *

By the time Ashley woke up, the sun was shooting fiery streaks onto her covers as it seared in through the cracks in the blinds. *Thank You, God, for air-conditioning.* Wait—she wasn't speaking to God.

Why was that, exactly? The only answer was that same feeling of oppressive loss she'd experienced last night. But her head didn't hurt and—

She sat up, her mind racing. She *remembered*.

Her parents—Ned and Rita. Her brother's name was Sam. Fumbling for her wallet, she dug out the picture again. Warmth flooded her chest as the memories filled her mind.

Sam and her at a theme park as kids—he'd been nearly two heads shorter than Ashley back then... Snowball fights—they'd grown up in Connecticut. Sandcastles at the beach... Sibling squabbles...

She grinned. Such good times.

But her heart twinged as she looked at his picture. Something had happened. But what? Sam was still in school, wasn't he? Or maybe he'd graduated before she'd moved to Washington.

When she'd gotten her dream job.

Ah, the irony of it all. She clapped a hand over her mouth, nearly giggling.

The call had come in the middle of dinner with her parents.

Congratulations, you've passed the background check. Your basic field training course starts in three weeks. Welcome to Quantico.

That was why she had the gun. She was an FBI special agent.

And she'd managed to finagle an assignment to the

coveted Washington field office. Years of work and effort finally paying off.

Yet none of it explained why she was here. And did the fake name mean it was an undercover assignment? Had she ever even gone undercover before?

Maybe her luggage held more clues.

She found a pair of yoga pants and a cotton T-shirt in one of her bags. After dressing, she pulled her long hair into a loose ponytail. She'd been so exhausted last night, what with all the wake-up calls, that she'd stumbled through a quick shower and fallen asleep on the couch without much thought. But now, looking in the mirror, she traced the lines of her face in the glass.

It was the face she had seen for a lifetime, familiar and yet not. Older. Because Ashley knew there was still a gaping blank spot—more like a chasm—behind that face. Places in her mind where the memories were gone, or maybe squished by swelling. Everything past the age of about twenty-six was blurry, faded into nothingness as she tried to recall anything more recent. But going by her birth date on the driver's license, she was twenty-seven.

That meant more than a year of her life was incomplete or missing.

After returning her wallet to the handbag, she walked out to the living room to dig through the luggage. The suitcase was full of clothing and toiletries—each item new, yet familiar, like muscle memory recalled the feel of each thing but her eyes were seeing them for the first time.

The other bag, a small satchel, was far more interesting. It held a laptop, a cell phone and an item that at first glance appeared to be a man's leather wallet. Upon flipping it open, it turned out to be her badge.

Special Agent Ashley Thompson, Federal Bureau of Investigation.

That was what she had tried to pull out of her pocket to show Logan yesterday as her proof for the gun.

But she had left the badge in her luggage.

Only one reason an agent wouldn't carry her badge. She must be working undercover. As a park ranger? Why here, in Big Bend?

Did any of them know she was an agent? Not Logan, obviously.

The laptop might tell her…

After three failed attempts at the password, the computer locked her out for the next hour. So much for that idea.

Plugging in the cell phone to recharge, she rummaged in the kitchen for anything edible. She found an apple and a bagel. Making a mental note to thank the receptionist, she scrolled through the contacts in the phone. Her finger hovered over her mom's cell phone number. One push and Ashley would hear a familiar voice.

No. She closed the contacts file. Calling anyone would be a great way to blow her cover. Plus, she had no reception out here anyway.

Instead she opened the phone's gallery. She scrolled through one image after another, watching a blur of faces fly past until one caught her eye. Sam, standing beside her, his arm slung around her shoulders.

The picture was time-stamped from last fall—just over a year ago. His wide grin made her want to smile but… Ashley furrowed her brows. Why did seeing him make her stomach twist?

She set the phone down and carried the cold, uneaten bagel to the kitchen before tackling the large suitcase. No point in dwelling on what she couldn't remember. Better to focus on what she *did* know—that she was a federal agent and she was in west Texas for a reason.

A reason that might have something to do with what had happened to her last night.

Wheeling the suitcase into her bedroom, Ashley slowly unpacked all the neatly folded clothing. Beneath the clothes, shoes and toiletries, she found a layer of books. A Bible, a couple of novels and a guide to desert animals and vegetation.

She thumbed through each one, placing them, in turn, on top of the dresser. When she got to the guidebook, as she flipped through pages of snakes and spiders and scorpions, a piece of paper fluttered out onto the floor.

She picked it up, noting the darkened, worn edges—as if someone had held it with dirty hands—and opened it carefully to reveal a full page of hand-drawn markings and tiny words.

A map. It was a map! A long, twisting river ran along the lower section with labeled towns on both sides. Strings of upside-down V's looked like mountain ranges and they were labeled, too. She almost needed a magnifying glass to read the letters. Or a lamp might help. She glanced up, suddenly noticing how dark it was—she'd been so absorbed with unpacking she hadn't looked at a clock in hours.

It must be getting late. Logan would be here soon to check on her.

She took the map into the living room, pausing to feel for a light switch, but in the momentary silence she heard a sound that made her blood run cold. A low scraping noise coming from the bedroom window, like someone was running a chisel between the casement and the wood frame. And it was far too rhythmic to be an animal or the wind.

Someone was trying to break into her house.

FOUR

Ashley's breath echoed loudly in her ears, her heart hammering, as she hastily folded up the map and tucked it inside the waistband of her pants. The sound persisted—*scratch, scratch, scratch*—and she tried to slow her breathing as she glanced around the room for a weapon.

She wanted her gun, but Logan had given it to the superintendent and he wouldn't return it until she was ready for duty. There—in the kitchen—the knife block. She crept through the dark living room and around the peninsula into the kitchen, pulling out one of the long knives at the top of the block.

The casement was moving now. The intruder struggled with the window, trying to pull it up as quietly as possible. With all the lights off, the trespasser probably thought she wasn't home. Her eyes darted to the front door. If she slipped outside now, whoever it was might never know she'd been in here.

But what if someone was waiting out there, too? Whoever had hit her in the head? And if the person at the window *was* working alone, she didn't want to miss her chance to identify the intruder.

Taking one slow, deliberate breath after another, she

crept to the doorway leading into the bedroom. She pressed her back against the living room wall and stole a glance around the doorjamb into the room. It was too dark to see who was outside the window, but gloved fingers worked underneath the inch-wide crack. If she had to pick, she'd guess they belonged to a man.

Her heart lurched. *Breathe. FBI agents don't panic.* They could wish for backup though, couldn't they?

Ashley's palms went slick with sweat. She tightened her grip on the knife handle as the window moved up another inch. She couldn't let him get all the way into the room or he might overpower her. But she wanted to see his face before she made a move.

Waiting was agony. Another inch and two hands appeared under the casement, now pushing together.

Almost time.

Somebody banged on the front door and Ashley was so startled she let out a cry. The hands disappeared from the window. That low, gritty brushing noise had to be retreating footsteps across the desert sand.

"Ashley?" Logan called, knocking again.

She dashed across the living room, throwing the door open. "Quick, around back. He's getting away."

Logan stared, his head cocked to one side. "What?"

She dropped the knife to the floor with a clatter and shoved past him, forgetting about her bare feet until she was already running around the back of the house. Even though the intruder might be long gone already, maybe she could still catch a glimpse of him. Anything that might give her a clue as to his identity.

"Where are you going?" he called, running after her. "You're supposed to be resting!"

Breathless, she stopped at the back corner of the building. Nobody. Nothing but an endless stretch of dirt, rocks and cactuses rolling toward the dark mass of the Chisos Mountains, barely visible against the sea of stars above.

He stopped next to her. "What's going on?"

Without a flashlight, it was pointless trying to run after the intruder. "A man was trying to break into my room, but you scared him off when you knocked."

"Are you all right?" Logan's resonant voice was full of concern.

"Yes, but I didn't get a description."

"Here." He pulled a flashlight from his pocket and flipped it on. "We can at least check for prints."

Of course he had a flashlight. Hers was sitting uselessly inside on the nightstand. Irritation sizzled through her veins but she forced herself to smile. "Glad you have a light."

"It's not very smart to wander around out here unprepared." The beam of light traveled across her feet, blindingly white against her black pants. "Or barefoot, for that matter. Don't you ever wear shoes?"

"It's not like I had time to lace up a pair of boots. And the river claimed the last pair. Let's look for footprints."

Logan held up his hand as she stepped toward the window. "No, you stay right there. You'll end up with your feet full of cactus spines, if they aren't already. Or worse, a rattlesnake bite."

Ashley opened her mouth to retort but then closed it, because now that he mentioned it, one of her feet did sting rather badly. But she wasn't about to tell him, so she watched silently as he waved the beam of light across the ground near the back of her house.

"Do you see anything?" she asked after a minute.

"Some crushed vegetation, but the dirt is bare and hard here. The window has been raised about two inches, though. We can dust for prints."

"He was wearing gloves."

"How do you know it was a man?" The beam of the flashlight obscured Logan's face.

"A hunch. The hands looked too large for a woman."

"Well, let's get you back inside." He shone the light on her feet again. "Can you walk?"

Ashley glared at him, even though he couldn't see her expression. "Of course. How do you think I got out here?"

"Oh, I saw it all. Just trying to be thoughtful."

"Well, you could at least light the path back for me."

He held out the light and Ashley picked her way carefully around to the front. Now that her body wasn't full of adrenaline anymore, her gaze snagged on the low-lying spiny plants and rocks. It was a wonder she hadn't tripped on them before. "Do you think there are rattlesnakes under any of those rocks?" she asked, trying to keep her voice even.

"Nah, not now. They come out at night to hunt, so they're more likely to be lying out in the open."

"You're just trying to scare me," she said hopefully.

"No, I'm not. But don't worry about the snakes. You're much more likely to step on a tarantula or a scorpion."

All those creepy pictures she had seen in the guidebook flooded into her mind. "I am?" She stopped, pulling up onto her tiptoes, as if that would help keep the spiders away.

"Sure. In fact, I think I see one right…there." He aimed the flashlight a little off to the left, and there, scuttling out from under a bush, was the largest, hairiest black spider she had ever seen.

Every muscle froze. Except her heart, which escaped into her throat along with a tiny scream. She'd rather face down a man breaking into her house any day. The tarantula crossed out of the beam of light, scuttling straight toward them. Whether out of self-preservation or sheer terror, Ashley flung her arm around Logan's neck and jumped.

He laughed, a rich, rolling sound, and easily caught her legs under the knees, until he was holding her against his chest. "You could've asked me to carry you."

"I...I," she stammered, her cheeks burning. "I *hate* spiders."

"Why exactly did you come to Big Bend, then?"

"That is the question, isn't it?"

The scent of pine trees and flannel emanated from his shirt, making her want to burrow into his arms for safety. She swallowed. What was wrong with her?

"I take it you haven't gotten back more of your memories yet?" Logan carried her around to the front of the house.

Why, *yes*, she had.

But until she learned why she was here and whom to trust, she had to keep things to herself. It would also help to know what her file here contained—surely the Bureau had invented some history for Ashley Watson. Whatever she told Logan had to match.

"Not really. Just some vague impressions. Maybe when I remember my laptop password, I'll figure out more." She hated lying to him, especially since he was the closest thing to a friend she had in the world right now.

They reached the front porch and the idea of letting the handsome ranger carry her across the threshold was more than she could take. She pushed against his chest and he released her gently onto her feet. "Thanks for the lift."

"Anytime. But—" he pointed down at her feet "—I don't want to see those bare feet again."

"Yes, Ranger Everett." She gave him a mock salute.

Logan stopped in the doorway, grinning at Ashley as she flipped on a light, picked up the knife she had dropped, and walked back into her house. She had a lot of nerve—he had to give her that. But he hated to think what might've happened if he hadn't come to her house when he had.

"What, exactly, were you going to do with that knife?" he asked casually.

She scowled. "Someone was breaking into my house, and you took away my gun. I needed some way to defend myself."

"You could've called for help."

"Like opened up the door and yelled?"

He shrugged. "It probably would've been enough."

"Probably?" Ashley dropped the knife into the kitchen sink and then walked—no, more like *hobbled*—into the living room. She must have stepped on something, after all.

"You can come in." She plopped onto her sofa and waved him into the living room. "Unless you think we'll be giving our neighbors the wrong impression."

He pulled away from the door and stepped inside, shutting it behind him. "No, someone tried to break in tonight. I think that warrants my being in here for now." He sat on a chair next to the sofa. "Do you have any idea what they wanted?"

Ashley's eyebrows pulled together for a moment but then she shook her head. "I'm not sure."

She was keeping something from him, no question.

Was it something she'd found today? Or remembered? And how to get it out of her? He ran a hand across his chin.

"It bothers me to think about you staying here alone," he said finally. "Maybe we should see about getting you into an apartment or staying with one of the families for tonight."

"No, I want to stay here. If he's stupid enough to come back, I want to see who it is."

He hadn't expected anything else. So much for worrying about giving the neighbors the wrong impression. Logan wasn't going to let her stay here alone. "Then I'm going to sleep on your sofa."

She leveled her dark brown eyes at him, as if weighing whether it was worth a battle. "Fine," she relented. "Suit yourself. But only for tonight, until I get my gun back."

"Agreed, on one condition."

"What?"

He pointed to her feet. "You let me check those for cactus spines."

Ashley frowned, pulling one foot up onto the opposite knee and leaning over to examine it. "I can do it myself."

Logan ran his hands through his hair. This woman was going to be a whole lot of trouble. "Is there a reason you can't accept my help?"

Maybe he was imagining things, but he could swear a pink tinge crept into those pale cheeks.

"You don't have to keep rescuing me." She stared at her foot. "I can pull my own weight."

"Ah." He waited until she looked up again. "You're afraid I'll think less of you."

She didn't say anything, but her cheeks turned a shade darker and she averted her eyes. She seemed so down-to-earth, so natural, sitting there with no makeup and her hair loosely pulled back. Unaware of how pretty she was.

"Ashley, I don't know why you're here, or how qualified or experienced you are, but I do know this—accepting help in a place like this is not a sign of weakness. The rangers here work as a team and we support each other. You and I are going to be spending a lot of time together, so you'd better get used to the idea."

She picked at her foot in silence for another minute before giving him a hesitant smile. "All right. I guess a pair of tweezers would help."

By the time she had retreated to her bedroom and Logan lay on the couch staring up at the dark ceiling, he could scarcely believe two hours had flown past. No more signs of the intruder, but he wasn't about to leave her alone.

Some mystery surrounded Ashley, lurking beneath the surface. Her file hadn't revealed anything insightful. But why would they assign her to Big Bend with no apparent experience in a similar environment? No ranger experience at all, in fact. Something wasn't adding up.

She had agreed to go with him to Santa Elena Canyon the next day, both to pick up her car and to see if anything jogged her memory. Until then, he had to find some way to fall asleep without thinking about the way Ashley had felt in his arms as he'd carried her back to the house. Even Erin, for all her inexperience as a new ranger, hadn't stirred such a strong protective instinct.

Maybe it was because five years had passed since Erin had left and Logan had changed during that time. He'd grown wiser. He'd seen more rangers come and go. He'd seen more loss and death.

Sam. That was who Ashley reminded him of. She didn't have quite the same youthful optimism and enthusiasm, but he could imagine she used to be that way. She certainly had the same energy, the same air of competence. Even some of their facial expressions were similar.

He rolled over on the couch for the twentieth time, wishing the government could afford better furniture. It made sense that Ashley would bring back all his memories of Sam—she was the first new law-enforcement ranger since his death.

But the thought of Ashley ending up with the same fate… He shuddered. He wouldn't let that happen, no matter how much she objected to his help.

It took another hour of prayer before he finally fell asleep.

FIVE

Ashley was relieved to find a note rather than a ranger in her living room the next morning. The events of last night had been awkward enough without waking up to share a cup of coffee and breakfast. She had felt horribly vulnerable in the last few days and now that her head was healing, it was time to reclaim some control over her life.

Logan's note indicated he wanted to get some things done before their drive to the canyon and that she could find him in his park office after her meeting with the superintendent.

She showered and dressed in one of the NPS uniforms in her closet; apparently they had been given to her when she'd arrived. More memories had solidified in her mind in the night, her past clicking back into place, giving her a reassuring sense of who she was and where she had come from.

But why she was here? Nothing. The previous months, except for that memory of a cab ride, were like staring at a blank wall.

She glanced at the time on the microwave. She had to meet with Dr. Barclay soon, but no harm in squeezing in another attempt at that laptop password. The last one she remembered hadn't worked yesterday. What else to try? Names of pets? Bobo the parakeet? Too short.

How about *JackyBoy*, after their chocolate lab?

Strike one.

College roommate? KristaReed.

Strike two.

She crinkled her nose. Only one chance left.

She closed her eyes, setting her fingers against the keyboard. Maybe muscle memory could pull out the password her conscious mind couldn't remember. It hovered right there, on the tips of her fingers. How about a hashtag first, for extra security?

Then... P-r-o-v— She stopped, rubbing her forehead.

Favorite Bible verse. Proverbs 3:5-6. But she would've abbreviated it. #Prov3:5-6.

Trust in the Lord with all thine heart, and lean not unto thine own understanding...

So painful to type, with the way the words seared her heart.

But it worked.

Ashley let out a little squeal of delight before sifting through the documents stored on the hard drive. Most of it seemed irrelevant, until she came across a file labeled "Big Bend." It contained several documents related to the park, including multiple maps and, better yet, several scanned pages of her own hand-written notes.

One name kept coming up over and over: Rico Jimenez. She shuddered. Somebody bad. But who was he?

She glanced again at the clock. Time to go. The superintendent was waiting. Tension crept into her shoulders as she hurriedly scanned the last few pages of notes. No doubt about it, she was here because of Jimenez. Now she had to figure out why.

Her gaze snagged on the message at the bottom of the last page, written in her own hand, as if her past self had left a warning. *Don't trust anyone.*

Anyone? Even the rangers? Logan? She shook her head, closing the laptop. Someone had tried to break into her house last night, and there were only two possible items she could think of that they might have wanted. This laptop or the map she'd found in the guidebook.

The map she would carry with her, but the laptop needed to be hidden. She left the case out in clear view but took the laptop itself and wedged it between the mattress and box spring in her bedroom, covering the gap with the sheets. It didn't seem likely anyone would try to break in during broad daylight, but better safe than sorry.

Ashley wanted to look at the map now, too, but she was out of time. Tucking it inside her shirt pocket, she walked the short distance to park headquarters.

The receptionist took her directly to the superintendent's office. Dick Barclay rose from his desk as she entered, shaking her hand.

"Good morning, Ranger Watson." He turned to the receptionist. "Sandy, please shut the door on your way out and see we're not disturbed."

Ashley took the seat opposite him. Wherever this conversation went, she'd have to be careful how much she revealed—at least until she knew whom to trust. One thing was sure: she'd have to downplay the extent of her memory loss if she didn't want to be sent packing.

"I'm glad to see you're feeling better," Barclay said. "Have you remembered yet what happened?"

"No, but I'm hopeful it will come back when we drive down to Santa Elena this afternoon. My older memories have almost fully returned." Only a slight stretch.

Barclay nodded, eyeing her thoughtfully. "Do you remember why you're here, Agent Thompson?"

Thompson. He knew she was undercover. That meant he must know about Jimenez, too. "Of course," she answered smoothly. "To catch Rico Jimenez."

Whoever he was.

Barclay sighed, pulling off his eyeglasses and rubbing the bridge of his nose. "This operation is a fool's errand. I tried telling Morton that two months ago."

The name clicked into place. Special Agent in Charge Donald Morton, her superior at the Bureau. She wiped her sweaty palms against her pants.

"I assure you, Dr. Barclay," she said, injecting her voice with as much confidence as she could, "that I'm quite capable of doing my job. It won't take long to apprehend Jimenez and bring him to justice."

Barclay leaned forward, elbows braced on his desk. "Agent Thompson, I don't know what happened to you yesterday, but this park has an incredibly low crime rate. I'm not going to let that change on my watch."

Her brow furrowed. A threat? Clearly, he didn't want her here. She forced a smile. "We're on the same side, Dr. Barclay."

His mouth pressed into a thin line. "Let me be blunt. There's no way Rico Jimenez or any other cartel leader is operating in this park under our noses. I didn't want you here before, and now that you've managed to injure yourself in your first twelve hours, I still don't want you here. My rangers are top-notch. We don't need FBI intervention."

She swallowed but held his gaze. "It would seem the Bureau doesn't agree. But I'll do my best to stay out of your way."

"You'll do more than that, Agent Thompson." Barclay's eyes narrowed. "You'll give me solid proof of Jimenez's activity, or else I'll call Morton and tell him about your memory loss."

"He'll send someone else."

He shrugged, one eyebrow rising over his wire-rimmed glasses. "But it won't be you." After a pause, he leaned forward in his seat. "Here's the thing. I agreed to this scheme as a favor to Morton, but I don't want any of you agents in my park. The sooner you get out of here, the better."

"Of course." She smiled, trying to exude the confidence she didn't feel. "I'll get you something soon."

"Three days." Barclay drummed his fingers on the desk. "I'll give you three days."

Not long, especially given the true extent of her memory loss. But Barclay didn't need to know that. She extended her hand. "No problem."

Barclay shook it firmly and rose. She stood, also. The interview certainly hadn't gone the way she'd hoped—putting her in the hot seat rather than revealing the crucial information she needed.

But as she turned to go, the superintendent held out a file. "Here's everything we've got on Jimenez. I hope it helps."

Was that sarcasm? Ashley took the file, resisting the urge to start looking through it on the spot and keeping back the thousand questions bursting to get out. "Do any of the other rangers know who I am?"

He shook his head. "Only myself and Ed Chambers."

"Thank you." She reached for the doorknob.

"Oh…and, Thompson? If you cause any trouble for me…"

She nodded, letting the rest of the threat go unspoken. "I won't, sir."

Do your job quickly, quietly, and get out. His eyes said all of it loud and clear.

Logan was working at his desk when someone knocked on the door. "Come in." He didn't bother to glance up.

"Good morning." *Ashley*.

At the sound of her voice, his heart skipped. He gritted his teeth. *Never should have carried her last night...* Not that she had given him much choice.

Erin had made his heart skip, too, almost from the first moment they'd met at headquarters. She'd been so young—twenty-three—cute and bubbly, full of energy. Fresh out of college. The world had held so much promise.

Now wasn't the time to dwell on the past, or the long years of heartache and loneliness Erin had left in her wake. Ed knew, but nobody else.

Work. Training the new ranger. Doing his job—that was why he was here. Every time he requested reassignment at Big Bend, it was because of this job and this place. *Not* because he was hoping for another Erin in his life. One was enough.

"Good morning." He forced himself to keep his eyes on his work a minute longer. Anything to help maintain a safe distance. "How are you feeling? Still up for a trip to Santa Elena?"

"I am," she said.

When Logan finally let himself look up, he was rewarded with wide, staring eyes and long, dark lashes. *Irrelevant*. "How did you sleep?" He rummaged under a stack of papers to find his keys.

"Better. I remembered my laptop's password."

"Really?"

She nodded but didn't say anything else. Just casually shifted her weight from one foot to the other. Secrets lurked behind those eyes. Maybe he'd be able to get answers this afternoon.

"The superintendent gave this to me for you." He handed Ashley her holster and gun, lips tilting. "Don't point it at me again."

A grin played at the corners of her mouth. "I won't."

He led the way out to the parking lot and as they stepped into the front lobby, Will Sykes came through the door.

Logan nodded in greeting, but Will stared at Ashley, the color leaching out of his naturally dark skin. Could Don Juan be nervous about meeting the new ranger, after all? Or did she remind him of Sam, too?

Ashley obviously didn't share his anxiety. She held out her hand, smiling. "Hello, I'm Ashley Watson."

Will recovered instantly, making Logan think he'd imagined it all. In fact, the younger man lavished such a warm smile on Ashley as he shook her hand that her cheeks turned rosy pink.

He was holding her hand far too long for a polite handshake. Logan cleared his throat. "Sykes, Ranger Watson and I need to get going."

Will gave Ashley another suave grin full of excessively white teeth. "Hope I'll see you around."

A few minutes later Logan steered the Jeep out onto the main road that would take them north and west around the Chisos Mountains and then south toward Santa Elena Canyon. Ashley stared at the landscape as if seeing it for the first time. Right—it'd been dark when he'd taken her on this road before, and her memories of driving out there were gone.

"Here, I brought you this." He handed her a park map. "I thought you might want to see where we're going."

"Thank you." The paper rustled as she spread it across her lap.

"So…what have you remembered?"

She laughed. "What are you looking for? My life story or something?"

"Sure, whatever you want to tell me. Maybe talking about it will help the rest of your memories come back."

"Maybe. I think I've got back everything up until about a year or so ago. After that, it's still pretty fuzzy."

"What about your family? You remember them? And where you came from?"

"What is this, Twenty Questions?" The sound of her laughter made his heart light. "Yes, I remember my parents. Ne—" She coughed, cutting herself short, almost as if she'd done it on purpose. But she picked back up almost immediately. "Never could forget them for long. One brother, too. His name is Sam."

"Older or younger?"

"Younger." She stared out the window for a long moment but when she turned back her eyes were bright. "He loves anything outdoors. He'd love it here."

Logan grinned. "Maybe you can invite him to visit sometime."

She smiled, but some of the excitement had faded.

Why? Already contemplating her escape from Big Bend?

They made the turn to the south, where the volcanic activity of ages long past had created what looked like a lunar landscape. Ashley stared out her window.

"I take it you don't remember seeing this scenery before?" he asked.

"No. I had no idea this park was so vast."

"Mountains, desert and river all rolled into one area. You could spend a lifetime here and never be done learning about it all."

"How long have you lived here?"

"It'll be seven years this fall." Five years since Erin had left. He hadn't heard from her since. But why was he thinking about Erin again? That chapter of his life was over.

"That's a long time to live somewhere so remote. Don't you miss civilization?" Ashley eyed him skeptically.

He couldn't help laughing at her expression. "Civilization's overrated. Besides, I love it out here, and the work I do is meaningful." God's will for his life. The knowledge that God had prepared him for this work was what had kept him going when Erin walked away.

"What about your family? Don't they miss you?"

"Sure." He shrugged, taking a deep breath. No avoiding the spiritual nudge to share his faith. "But they're glad I'm following God's call for my life." He waited for the awkward silence, or worse, the ridicule he usually received when he talked about his faith.

But Ashley smiled. "You're a Christian, aren't you?"

"Since childhood. Although I haven't always walked faithfully with the Lord."

"Me, either." She was silent for a long moment. "I wish… I wish it was easier to understand God's plans."

"Sometimes things don't make sense until we look back on them later. I guess that's why so many people in the Bible were commended for walking by faith not sight." A lesson he needed to remind himself about. Maybe even his broken heart would make sense one day.

"Maybe." Her voice sounded hard now, almost bitter. Was it because of the memory loss and her confusion over what had happened to her? Something else? Pain lingered there, but it wasn't his business.

Ashley stared back out the window. He wanted to ask her more questions, about what she had remembered, or whether she had requested this assignment at Big Bend. But the timing seemed all wrong. So instead he changed the subject, spending the next half hour teaching her about safety and survival in the desert. Barely the tip of the iceberg, but he'd keep going over it every day until he'd drilled it into her head.

They were nearing the road to the canyon, but first he turned into the parking lot at Castolon.

"Why are we pulling in here?" Ashley asked.

"We had your car towed here for safe-keeping. Rangers are stationed at Castolon, but Santa Elena is only monitored by patrols."

He parked the Jeep next to her black sedan, which had been left in the lot outside the general store, ice-cream stand and restrooms.

"Apparently it didn't work," she said grimly, "because one of the rear windows has been broken out."

Logan frowned as he watched her get out of the Jeep. First her house and now the car.

What did Ashley have that somebody wanted?

SIX

The backseat was littered with fragments of broken glass, bits of leaves and windblown sand. Ashley climbed into the driver's seat.

"Is anything missing?" Logan's face was lined with concern.

"I don't know." She opened the glove compartment and rummaged through the contents. Anything to shake this nagging sense of vulnerability. "I thought I took out all of my personal belongings when we left it behind, but maybe I missed something."

"The trunk was empty when we left it." His brows pulled together. "Maybe it was the same person who tried to break into your house."

Probably so. But this wasn't the kind of proof she was looking for to give Barclay. Although she couldn't remember getting the car, it had to be a rental set up through the Bureau using her fake name. Now she'd have to explain the damage to Special Agent Morton, who didn't even know yet about the incident in the river. A knot of frustration twisted in her stomach.

Logan pulled out a handheld radio and made a call. Ashley only half paid attention as she walked around the car, inspecting it for other signs of damage.

"One of the Castolon rangers is going to come take a look and talk to Jim at the general store to see if he's noticed anything suspicious." Logan nodded toward the west where, far off in the distance, puffy, white cotton-ball clouds floated on the horizon. "Storm's coming this way. We should get down to the canyon while we still have time. We can pick up the car on the way back. Jim will make sure the window gets taped up."

"All right." Wasn't much they could do about the car anyway. Even if they picked over the interior with a fine-toothed comb and dusted for prints, she doubted they'd find anything helpful. Like the break-in at her house, there was no way of knowing who it was or what they wanted.

"So—" he started the Jeep once she got in "—what were they after?"

"Probably whatever they were trying to find in my house." *Like that map.* Or maybe the truth about who she was? Did someone else in the park suspect she was an FBI agent?

Instead of backing out, Logan scanned her face. "Do you have any ideas? Maybe something you brought with you?"

She shrugged. "Your guess is as good as mine. My computer, maybe?"

"We're a little remote for petty theft, but maybe." He kept those green eyes pinned on her until Ashley couldn't bear it any longer.

She stared out the window at the old, stucco ice-cream stand, its log roof beams protruding from nubby textured walls. He could see right through her evasive answers— see that she was keeping secrets—and even though she barely knew him, she hated the deception. But until she knew whom to trust, she didn't have a choice.

Finally he threw the Jeep into reverse and pulled onto the road. The sun was now high enough overhead that heat radiated off the asphalt in shimmering waves, creating a mirage around every turn. According to the map, they'd pass Cottonwood Campground next and then have another six miles or so to the Santa Elena parking lot.

Probably the wrong time to pry for information, but she needed whatever she could get. Plus, the awkward silence was driving her nuts. "Can I ask you something?"

"Sure. Anything."

He sounded like he genuinely meant it. He'd been nothing but kind, helpful and concerned, and she had only repaid him with silence and secrets. Guilt twisted her insides.

She swallowed her self-condemnation. "What *are* the typical crimes we have to deal with here? If it's not petty theft and breaking and entering."

"Thankfully we're remote enough there isn't much crime, but as you might remember from your dip in the river, it's very shallow. The ease of crossing the border is the real issue. Even then, the most we usually see are a couple of Mexicans illegally crossing over to sell trinkets to tourists. We've had a few drug busts, but nothing large scale."

"What about illegal immigration? Human trafficking?"

"Not so much. Most of the cartels operate to the west of here, where the terrain is less rugged. You've probably heard of Organ Pipe Cactus National Monument in Arizona. The rangers there have constant issues with border crossings."

Ashley *had* heard of it—at least, somewhere in her memory, she knew there was a connection with ranger deaths there and something to do with her work here.

Maybe later, when she had time to dig through the files on her laptop, she'd find more answers.

Logan drove the Jeep over a dry streambed and pulled into the parking lot at Santa Elena. She followed him in silence across a flat plain toward the trailhead into the canyon. The air felt slightly less oppressive here, closer to the river, and a breeze danced through the stray bits of hair falling around her face.

The Rio Grande had cut a deep canyon through a high plateau, leaving jagged cliffs on either side. Mexico was only a stone's throw away, a sheer cliff face towering hundreds of feet above the water. On the US side, a narrow path had been carved along the edge of the river, with steps rising and then dropping to the river's edge where the canyon widened. Vegetation grew here and there along the path, cactuses along the upper portion and tall grasses and brush down along the gravelly riverbank.

They had walked a short distance into the canyon when Logan stopped. "Anything look familiar?"

"Nothing other than the reeds and the river's edge, but that's because I remember it from crawling out." She stared down the trail, studying the undulations of the path and the way it hugged the cliff face at some points, veering back toward the river at others.

"Well, let's keep going." Logan glanced at the sky and then at his watch, the type that looked like it could endure a hurricane and still tell the time, temperature and direction of true north. "We don't have much more time."

"I'm not lying to you," she called after him as he started back up the trail. At least, not directly. Did withholding the truth count as lying?

"Never said you were." He kept walking without looking back, but his voice didn't carry much conviction.

"Please, Logan." Guilt and frustration compressed her

chest like a heavy weight. It was bad enough having a hole in her mind, but for him to think badly of her, too… Well, his opinion mattered to her more than it should. "I can't remember what happened here."

He walked on in silence for a few more minutes, until the path had reached a height above the river from which she never could have fallen and survived. He stopped and pointed to the water. "There's no way you could've fallen in there by accident from this path."

"I know." She pressed a hand to her chest, looking over the edge of the cliff. It would be a long, steep, cactus-filled tumble to the river from this height.

"Ashley, why were you even out here? On your first day, why would you have driven to this canyon?"

She shook her head miserably. "I have no idea."

He placed both hands on her shoulders, pinning her with his steady gaze. "I want to believe you. But how can I help you when you won't tell me anything?"

She opened her mouth to object but realized she had nothing to say to him. Again.

His eyes, now a deep green in the shade of the canyon wall, scanned her face, as if he were trying to read her soul. "You've remembered more than you're telling me."

She swallowed, seized with the sudden urge to break free of his scrutiny and escape. "I *don't* remember asking for your help."

He raised an eyebrow. "You didn't seem to mind last night, when you leaped into my arms."

Of all the nerve. Her cheeks flamed instantly and this time she twisted free from his hands, still warm and heavy on her shoulders. "Your job, Ranger Everett, is to train me as a Big Bend ranger. Not pry into my personal life."

"Fine." He stepped past her, back in the direction they

had come. "In that case, we're done here, because I don't want to be trapped with you on this side of the stream-bed when the rain comes."

This day hadn't gone anything like Logan planned, and the way Ashley was withholding information rubbed him the wrong way. After all his years in law enforcement, he'd learned to read people well enough to know when they were keeping secrets.

Sure, she had every right to hold back details about her personal life, but her reasons for being here were park business. His business. And her stubborn refusal to talk to him about it—to trust him—was just frustrating.

He stalked along the trail without looking back. It had been a fool's errand anyway—something he'd suspected before they'd even taken the trail. But he'd hoped she would remember something or open up about what she already knew—anything to give him some clues.

The clouds rolled closer, intermittently blotting out the sun, and the scent of impending rain danced in the air. They were running out of time to get across the stream-bed before it flooded. He picked up the pace but slowed again when they reached the most dangerous part of the trail, where the canyon narrowed and the path clung tenaciously to the cliff face above a long, rocky fall to the river below.

Suddenly a sharp, deafening crack split the air and a spray of rocks pelted the side of his face. He jerked around, his eyes meeting Ashley's stunned brown ones.

"What…?" she asked.

Too close for thunder. Too brief for a rockslide.

The crack came again, along with another burst of rocks between them, but this time he heard the telltale whizzing sound, too.

"Down!" he yelled, jumping toward Ashley and all but tackling her to the dirt path as another bullet zinged over their heads. "Someone's shooting at us!"

Dirt and rocks bit into his hands as he pushed himself up. Based on the angle of the bullet into the canyon, the sniper was shooting from the Mexican side.

Ashley scrambled onto her knees, pulling her gun and firing off a random shot across the river. Another crack, along with the glint of sunshine off metal at the top of the opposite cliff. Dirt sprayed near her head. That one was way too close.

"We're sitting ducks up here. We've got to get down." Logan shoved her ahead and pulled out his gun, firing in the direction of the gunman and hoping they weren't creating an international incident.

Ashley was sure-footed and nimble as she raced ahead of him, dodging rocks and spiny plants cluttering the edges of the narrow path. Despite the business suit and his earlier assumptions, she was obviously in top physical condition.

Another loud clap reached his ears as they sprinted across the sand toward the parking lot. Thankfully the Jeep was the only vehicle in the lot. At least they didn't have to worry about protecting tourists, too.

"What kind of range does that weapon have?" she called.

"That wasn't a gunshot," he said as they reached the Jeep. "That one was thunder." He grabbed for his door handle but jerked back as a split-second later the Jeep's windshield shattered.

"And that was a bullet." Ashley dove for the pavement behind the Jeep.

He crouched beside her as another bullet ricocheted off the vehicle's hood. "There have to be two shooters.

The one in the canyon couldn't clear the angle to reach us here."

"Unless he's running like we are," she panted, eyes sparking. "I thought you said there weren't many border incidents here."

"There weren't, until you arrived."

"What do we do now?"

As if in response, lightning flared bright, followed by a boom so loud it made the ground vibrate. To the west, the dark clouds loomed ever closer, even though the sky was still a breathtaking blue in the east.

"We're running out of time before the streambed floods."

"The one we drove over?" Ashley stared across the parking lot at the large yellow sign that warned tourists not to cross in flood conditions. "How much rain do you think we're going to get?"

"Doesn't take much. A couple of inches in a sudden downpour is enough to flood the streambed and arroyos."

She nodded, but her eyes had grown wide. So, a sniper didn't scare her, but the power of nature apparently did.

"Hey." He reached across the space between them and squeezed her cold hand. "God's in control here, remember? Whatever happens."

Ashley exhaled. "You get the Jeep started. I'll cover you."

She disappeared around the side of the vehicle, firing shots back across the river. Logan fumbled for the keys, waited a second longer and then dashed around the driver's side, throwing open the door and ducking behind it as a bullet lodged into the metal body of the Jeep.

He slipped the key into the ignition and turned it, keeping his head low as he climbed into the seat. The engine cranked to life and Ashley jumped in beside him.

He threw the vehicle into Reverse, backing across the lot to escape the gunner's range.

He tossed her the radio as he put the Jeep in Drive, heading for the road and the streambed. "Call this in, okay?"

She pressed the talk button and made the report as the first drops of rain fell. Without windows, it would be a matter of minutes before they were soaked.

Ashley finished the call and stuffed the radio under the seat. "Marfa border control is sending a helicopter to look for the gunmen."

"It'll be too late." Logan shook his head. But what else could they do?

Rain spattered on the vehicle's metal hood, kicked up dust on the road and filled the air with a hot, wet smell.

He pulled the Jeep onto the main road as another loud crack rent the air. He and Ashley both ducked, but the shot hit somewhere in the back of the Jeep. Another clap sounded right behind them and this time the Jeep lilted ominously toward the passenger side as the rear tire blew. Logan slammed his foot on the gas anyway. They just needed to get out of the shooter's range…

More shots, but finally they were falling short, striking the road and rebounding off the asphalt. Vicious shrieking sounds of grinding metal came from the back of the Jeep, so Logan eased off the gas and let the vehicle roll to a stop.

In the streambed.

He clenched his teeth together. It couldn't be helped.

"Are we out of range yet?" Ashley asked as a bright flash of lightning lit the dark sky. A loud clap of thunder followed close behind, but no more gunshots.

"Think so. But this vehicle isn't going any farther." He climbed out of the Jeep and checked the rear tire.

Completely deflated, its warped rim resting on the road. Hopefully the axle wasn't so bent it couldn't be driven. "Tire's blown," he called over the pounding rain.

Ashley stepped up beside him, rain droplets streaking down her pale face and dripping off her eyelashes as she blinked at the yellow warning sign fifty feet away.

He squeezed her arm then turned away to the Jeep's tailgate. Time to see how fast he could change a tire.

SEVEN

Ashley clutched her gun tightly, although it wasn't going to help against a flood. Instinct demanded she run, but that was panic talking. Because then what would they do? Run all the way back to Castolon?

"We've gotta try." Logan dug in the back of the Jeep for a toolbox. "Somebody over there is trying to kill us, and if he decides to cross the river and get closer, his aim is going to get a whole lot better."

He was right, of course. "What do you want me to do?" Her voice was hoarse from yelling over the din of the storm.

Taking out a wrench, he detached the spare tire from the rear gate. "Cover me. And watch the streambed. It only takes twelve inches of water to wash away a car."

"That's not very comforting." She crouched beside the Jeep as Logan wedged a jack under the rear axle.

Water trickled past them, running in narrow channels through the hard, dusty ground, forming puddles in low places and soaking through the knees of her pants. Lightning filled the darkening sky. It was followed by a clap of thunder so loud, she jumped in surprise.

How many inches of water did it take to sweep a person away?

Logan was halfway under the Jeep now, pulling off the old tire. No gunshots, no sign of the shooter. But at that moment, the heavens opened and buckets of water poured down so hard it obscured their visibility.

In a matter of seconds water swirled around her boots, carrying sticks and leaves and candy wrappers from miles upstream. How many inches were there now? Three? Her hands shook. A shooter was predictable, to a degree, and things that could be predicted could be controlled. But not this…not the fury of nature unleashed on the earth.

Only God could control that and He didn't appear interested.

She watched in mute horror as the water seeped in through the lace holes and around the tongue of her boots, soaking her socks. Surprisingly cold given the hot day. How much longer could they wait?

Logan pulled out from under the Jeep, yanking her arm as he stood. "We have to get out of here!" he yelled over the noise of the storm. "Now!"

"What about the Jeep?"

"No time. Go!"

He snatched her hand, tugging her as he ran toward the far side of the streambed. The water swirled around their ankles and kept rising fast.

The current ripped past her feet, so strong for so little water. It couldn't be more than four inches deep.

"Come on!" Logan yanked on her arm.

Her feet vanished beneath the dark, muddy stream. And the rain, pouring down in dog-size drops, made it hard to even see which direction they were running. *Stay perpendicular to the current.* She clung to the thought as if it were a lifeline.

Logan gripped her hand so hard it hurt. The dark

water whirled above her ankles now, a vicious torrent threatening to sweep them away at the first misstep. Like a far deadlier version of the river she had been in a few days ago.

Only, this time, she might not be so fortunate.

"Almost there," Logan huffed.

Finally the water became shallower, making their steps easier. They reached the far side and clambered onto the bank. Ashley staggered forward a few extra paces to give the rushing stream a wide berth. Then Logan released his death grip on her hand and they both flung themselves to the muddy ground.

She lay on her side, heaving in several deep breaths as the rain continued to pour down. When she had finally recovered enough to sit, she stared at the Jeep, where they had been kneeling on the ground only moments before.

The muddy water had reached the doors and was flowing into the cab. She hugged her arms around her chest, painfully aware of her own helplessness as the now roaring current tore loose items from the Jeep and carried them away. Seconds later the Jeep itself rocked as a torrential flow of water rushed through the once-dry creek bed. Suddenly, as if pushed by a large, invisible hand, the vehicle overturned and was gone, carried by the ripping current toward the Rio Grande.

Ashley stared at the place the Jeep had stood, open-mouthed, hands trembling. She had never seen nature's fury like this before. It was as if the hand of God had reached down and touched the earth in front of her eyes. If they had stayed there a few seconds longer… The thought sent a chill down her back until, combined with her wet clothes, she shivered from head to toe.

* * *

She was shaking uncontrollably. It was a gut reaction. Before Logan could stop himself, he pulled Ashley into his arms, as if he could will away the cold and the fear by holding her close. Her breath whispered warm against his arm, the cold wet of her cheek slowly giving way to heat. Her dark hair had come loose and fell like a heavy, wet blanket down her back.

At least no one was taking shots at them anymore. But given the downpour, and the flooding, there was no way they would ever find the shooters.

No, there was only one source for answers in that regard. He gazed down at Ashley, her forehead so pale against her dark hair. Maybe now she would be willing to open up. To let him help.

Too soon Ashley pushed against him, her hand on his chest. He hated to let go. She felt too warm, too safe. But theirs was a working relationship and he couldn't afford the tangle of emotions in his chest. Not after Erin.

Logan dropped his hands and Ashley pulled away, her wide eyes filled with confusion and lingering fear that, despite his resolve, he longed to soothe away.

Instead he summoned all his effort and looked back across the streambed. The rain had stopped and the sun was forcing its way through the dark clouds in glittering brilliant streaks. The rushing water next to them slowed and began to recede now that its source had moved east.

"I'm sorry," he ground out, "that I didn't get us out of there sooner."

"It's not your fault." Ashley reached for him, her cold hand resting lightly on his arm. Although her hands still trembled slightly, the color had returned to her cheeks. "We had to try. At least no one can follow us across the creek at the moment."

Logan ran his hands through his hair, sending out a spray of water, trying to clear his head. "The radio's halfway to the Gulf of Mexico by now. We'll have to walk." They were going to get thirsty, but at least the day carried a hint of cooler fall temperatures, instead of the torturing three-digit heat they'd had all summer. He glanced at Ashley, worry gnawing at his insides. "You shouldn't be exerting yourself like this while you're still healing."

She shrugged, her dark eyes calm. "Headquarters got my call. They'll send somebody. But walking sounds better than sitting around here without any shade. And, honestly, I feel pretty good except for the memory loss."

He nodded, pressing his lips together. "Well, I'm not happy about it, but you've got a point."

They started up the road toward Castolon. It felt good to stretch his stiff muscles as he walked, keeping the pace easy for Ashley. The sun was gaining strength again and slowly drying out their clothes and hair.

She strolled silently beside him, staring at the road ahead.

He kept stealing glances to make sure she was all right, until finally she gave him a crooked grin. "Logan, I'm okay. Obviously, I only remember bits and pieces about the last year, but I must've exercised regularly. I feel *fine*."

He frowned, watching the remains of the puffy gray clouds as they disappeared to the east. "It's not just the exertion I'm worried about. First you turn up in the river with a head injury, then your house and your car are broken into, and now someone is shooting at us. Whatever is going on here, *you* are at the center of it. Do you have any idea why?"

* * *

Yes, she did. It took a major effort to swallow the word before it popped out. The effect this man had on her was almost more frustrating than her lost memories. Ashley wanted nothing more than to tell him everything and crawl into the safety of his arms.

Her heart wanted to trust him implicitly, but logic dictated that was foolish. She hardly knew him. And her own words before coming here were to trust no one. That *had* to include Logan.

But he was waiting for her to say something and she owed it to him after putting his life in jeopardy. Though she didn't know who'd been shooting at them, she had no doubt the incident was linked to Jimenez. Did that mean her cover was blown? Before she'd even had the chance to remember everything?

Regardless, she wasn't about to admit defeat yet.

She couldn't tell Logan she was with the FBI or searching for Rico Jimenez, but maybe she could tell him about the map. Maybe he could even help her figure out why it was important.

She sucked in a deep breath, letting it out slowly. "I think I might know what they want."

He raised an eyebrow. "What?"

She unbuttoned the flap on her shirt pocket, pulling out the now rather damp piece of paper she had carried with her all day. Gingerly she unfolded the map, smoothing the rumpled corners.

Logan leaned closer, looking over her shoulder, and every nerve flared to life at his nearness. *Not* what she was supposed to be thinking about.

"I think it's a map, but I haven't had time to study it yet."

He ran his hand over his chin. "Where did you find it?"

"Tucked into a guidebook I brought with me." She glanced up at him, right into those green eyes that made her think of pine trees and snowcapped mountains and cozy ski lodges. Her breath stuck in her throat. Good-looking, kindhearted and selfless. A wonder he wasn't married yet. *Focus. Not important details.* "What do you think it is?"

"Honestly, it looks like Big Bend. This—" he pointed at different features as he spoke "—is the Rio Grande. And here are the Chisos Mountains. Elephant Tusk. Mariscal Mountain. The hot springs. Boquillas Canyon. Whoever made this knew the area well."

"And this is Mexico?" She pointed to the area south of the river.

He nodded. "There are a couple of small villages out here—Santa Elena, San Vicente, Boquillas. But most of this area is a nature preserve protected by the Mexican government. The nearest big city is Ojinaga, across the border from El Paso."

"Look, it's dated. Right here—1567." She pointed at the tiny numbers written near the text.

Logan's brow wrinkled. "The paper seems old, but not *that* old."

"It could be a copy, couldn't it?" Ashley squinted at the tiny letters. "This writing… Is it Spanish?"

"Looks like it. I have a dictionary in my office. And you don't have any idea where you got it from?"

Something about the map—maybe the way the paper felt in her hand—tugged at her memory. "I remember…" She paused, trying to seize the vague impressions in her mind. "I remember opening an envelope. The map was inside. Something about it made me feel…sad."

She tried to picture that moment in her mind. If only she could remember when it had happened and the return address on the envelope. But wait—the envelope hadn't been marked with a return address, had it?

It had only borne her name and address, and the post office's cancellation. From…

"Panther Junction." She snapped her eyes up to his. "It was posted from Panther Junction. There's a post office, isn't there?"

He nodded. "It's the only one in the park. When did you get it in the mail?"

She thought for a moment. "It was recent. One of the last things I remember before waking up on the river-bank."

"Who would send you a map of Big Bend?"

"No idea." She shrugged helplessly. And, more important, how was this map linked to Jimenez?

"So, what's it for?"

She stared at the writing again as the hot sun scorched the top of her head. Probably time to refold the map and give up. *Wait*—a written phrase caught her eye. "Look—" she pointed above one of the mountain peaks "—there's a notation here in English. And the handwriting is different. It says 'lost mine.'"

"Sure, it's called Lost Mine Peak. Second in height behind Emory Peak."

"But look here, at this symbol—*Au*. It's written in the same handwriting."

Logan squinted at the map. "So?"

"Gold. It's the symbol for gold, from the periodic table."

"How do you know it's referring to the periodic table?"

"And here," she persisted. "'Mariscal.' It's a mine, too, right? I remember seeing it on the map you gave me."

"Hg," he murmured.

"Mercury. It was a mercury mine, wasn't it?"

He nodded. "First half of the twentieth century. It produced nearly a quarter of the country's mercury."

Ashley glanced over her shoulder, making sure the road was still empty. "Logan, what if this map shows the location of a gold mine right here in Big Bend?"

Logan stared, vaguely aware that his mouth was hanging open. *Rookie.* "Right there on Lost Mine Peak? It's just a name, Ashley. Hundreds of places in the west are named after lost mines."

"You're an expert on Big Bend, right?" Her dark eyes narrowed. "Aren't there any legends about lost mines?"

"Well, sure, but there are also legends about lost canyons full of bison, and we haven't found any of those yet, either."

She stared at him, waiting.

He tugged at his shirt collar, hot now that his clothes had dried out. "We'd better keep walking. Still have a few miles to go."

She folded the map and returned it to her shirt pocket. "Tell me one of the legends. You've got to know one. In fact, I bet you know one about Lost Mine Peak, don't you?"

"Maybe. You're not going to drop it, are you?"

"No." A grin lit up her face, making her eyes sparkle. "I'm very persistent."

He sighed. "The legend says that back in the 1500s—"

"Fifteen sixty-seven!" she said triumphantly. "That's the date on this map!"

He scowled before continuing, as if she hadn't interrupted. "The Spanish found a rich vein of gold near the top of Lost Mine Peak. They hauled life-term prisoners twenty miles across the desert from the presidio at San Vicente, blindfolded part of the way, to work the mine."

"That must've been miserable." She frowned. "What happened?"

"The Comanche, angry over the Spanish invasion of their lands, found the mine and killed all the workers, to a man. Then they filled in the entrance to hide it from anyone else who might come looking."

"And you don't think it could be true?"

"Well... I guess if I'm being objective, the Chisos Mountains are igneous rock formations, so theoretically it's possible there could be veins of gold. It just seems so...improbable."

She stared across the desert at the mountains in the north. "Apparently whoever made this map doesn't agree with you."

"And the people trying to get it from you?" He raised an eyebrow. How could he believe such a ridiculous theory? Still, there was no denying someone wanted *something* from her.

Ashley nodded.

"And you think the people after the map are the ones who threw you into the river?"

"I have no idea. But it's my best guess. Somehow they found me in the park, realized I didn't have the map, and dumped me into the river."

When she put it like that... He swallowed, his stomach flipping. The thought of some thug attacking her, searching her and throwing her into the river like a piece of trash... It made him want to find whoever had done it and bring them to justice. Maybe after he knocked a couple of teeth out.

She was still pale, whether from the same line of

thought or from the incident by the river, he didn't know. But she needed help.

Or to get out of Big Bend.

"It's not safe for you here," he said at last. "You should leave the park. Turn that map over to Ed Chambers and the superintendent and let them sort it out. I'm sure they could get you a transfer." Even if the thought of her leaving twisted uncomfortably at his heart, her safety was more important.

"I can't." She clenched her teeth.

"Why?"

She shook her head. "Don't ask, because I don't know all the reasons yet myself. I only know that I can't leave."

He ran a hand through his hair. "At least turn the map over to the superintendent. If the NPS sends rangers out searching for this mine, then maybe whoever is after the map will give up."

"Aren't you at all concerned about finding whoever it is and arresting them? We *are* in law enforcement, aren't we?"

He stopped and, before he quite knew what he was doing, gently gripped both of her arms and stared into her dark eyes. "Of course. But I'm more concerned about protecting you."

Confusion flickered across her face—warmth mingled with wariness, as if she couldn't make up her mind.

For a moment Logan didn't know what she would do, or what he wanted her to do—step into his arms or walk away. The latter would certainly be better for his sanity.

She did neither. Instead she stood like a statue, saying in a clipped voice, "I'm here to do a job. I don't need your protection."

Worse than a slap in the face. He pulled his hands

back, retreating a step. With a curt nod, he walked ahead in silence.

It seemed obvious Ashley needed his help—someone had tried to shoot them, after all. So why was she pushing him away? Either she had a chip on her shoulder the size of Montana about accepting help or…he was letting things get too personal, and she could tell.

And it was obvious she didn't want any part of his unruly emotions.

Logan kicked a rock on the road as they trudged on under the hot sun. He barely knew Ashley. It had been… what, three days since they had met? Why did it feel like so much longer?

He had to get his feelings back under control, take them out of the picture. View her for what she was—a coworker who needed training. Not an attractive, mysterious, brave woman who needed his protection.

He could turn off his heart. Somehow.

EIGHT

Pressing a washcloth to her face, Ashley scrubbed away the grime, wishing she could wash away all the fear and uncertainty inside just as easily. The past three days had lasted an eternity.

After they'd walked a long way, a ranger had picked them up and given them a lift back to Castolon. From there, she and Logan had driven her car to Panther Junction. He'd kept teaching her about the park as they'd driven: its layout, wildlife, policies…anything to avoid the uncomfortable looming silence. Despite her admittedly cold words to him earlier in the day, Logan had insisted on checking her house to make sure no one had broken in, before leaving for his office.

She had to give him credit for his work ethic. Long hours, flexibility and dedication were a given with the Bureau, but the working conditions weren't typically quite this…wet. Or sandy. After all they'd been through, all she'd wanted was a shower.

And some time alone to figure things out.

After throwing on a pair of blue jeans and a black T-shirt, she retrieved her laptop and carried it out to the living room. She flipped it open, finding the file with her notes.

Two more days. She had two more days to come up with some sort of information for Dick Barclay—something to convince him not to call Morton. She had no doubt what would happen if her boss found out about the memory loss—she'd be on the next flight home.

Ashley rested her chin on her hand. It would help, obviously, if *she* knew why she was there. Why this place, and this map, mattered. Although Dick Barclay knew she was with the FBI, and here to investigate Jimenez, he didn't seem to know about the map or the gold mine—otherwise he would have mentioned them.

Unless… She tapped her chin. What if Barclay hadn't wanted to remind her about it?

No, that was ridiculous. Barclay had only been here… what? Six months? How could he know about the mine when not even Logan did?

The map was connected to this case somehow, though. Maybe it was the lead that had brought her here. Maybe the cartel was searching for the mine, too, and if she found it, she'd find Jimenez.

Or maybe she was desperate and grasping for straws. She'd be able to concentrate a whole lot better if she could stop thinking about Logan. She had hurt his feelings today, that was obvious, but it was safer this way. When she didn't know whom she could trust, or what tomorrow might bring, it was too dangerous to let him in. Just being around her had put him in physical danger.

And no matter how rational Ashley tried to be about him, her stubborn heart wasn't listening. He had held her so closely this afternoon, and the last thing her heart had wanted was for him to let go.

Even now, that same foolish part of her wanted him to knock on the door. To listen to her, help her, keep her safe.

"Absolutely not," she muttered aloud. She'd worked too long and too hard to succeed in a man's world, and she wasn't about to turn herself into a needy, withering female just because a good-looking, good-hearted man had rescued her once or twice. Or three times. She was beginning to lose count.

Ashley turned back to her notes, forcing her mind to concentrate on the screen in front of her. There were those words again—the best reason not to let Logan Everett too close. *Trust no one.*

Why? She scanned page after page and then she found it. A reference to an FBI report on Jimenez's suspected criminal activity in the Big Bend country. *Please let it be here on this computer.*

Oh, happy day, there it was. Finally something was going her way. The document claimed Jimenez had split off from a large cartel in western Mexico, starting his own operation a couple of years ago. He or his men had a long string of associated violent crimes linked to drug running and serving as coyotes for illegal immigrants.

But what would Jimenez want with Big Bend? The river was shallow here, making crossings easier, and the area was understaffed. Yet the terrain was so rugged, it would be nearly impossible to move drugs or people safely into the States on a large scale. So what *was* Jimenez doing in Big Bend?

According to the file, the Bureau had a contact in San Vicente who'd reported on Jimenez. Small drug runs. Cartel members moving back and forth across the border… Was it related to the mine? And how was he doing it undetected?

Obviously, Logan hadn't heard anything about the cartel. Even the superintendent didn't think Jimenez was working in the area, if the file he had given her was any indication.

Ashley shivered as the answer came to her. Of course. Someone on the inside was helping him. It could be border patrol or the local authorities or someone right here with the NPS. Whoever it was, they were orchestrating Jimenez's movements to pass unnoticed.

At that thought, memories of conversations with Morton back in his DC office flooded into her mind. *That* was why she was here undercover—not only to avoid scaring off Jimenez, but because the FBI suspected it was one of the Big Bend rangers. And it was her job to figure out whom, along with pinning Jimenez.

Something else niggled at the edge of her memory. She couldn't shake the feeling that this specific assignment was personal. She'd fought to convince Morton she was the right agent. But why?

Ashley patted her jeans' pocket, where she'd tucked the map safely away. It had to have something to do with this map. What? And why had someone sent it to her? She rubbed her hands across her face, straining to dredge up any other memories that might help.

A sudden knock on the door interrupted her and Ashley's shoulders tensed. It had to be Logan. She wasn't ready to face him again yet, not now. He seemed so good, so trustworthy… The thought of him being the traitor, however unlikely, made her stomach hurt.

The knock came again and she closed her laptop. Her lights were on, so it was obvious she was home. She couldn't hide forever.

Only, it wasn't Logan. It was Will Sykes, the ranger she had met this morning.

"Hi, Will," she said. With his dark good looks and

charming smile, he might've chosen a career in Hollywood instead of life in remote Big Bend.

"Ashley." He flashed a wide grin. "I heard you had some sort of crazy incident down at Santa Elena this afternoon."

"Yeah." Did every ranger know by now? "It was a little more than I bargained for on my first day of work."

"I bet." He leaned casually against the door frame, his dark eyes unreadable. "Hey, didn't you have some sort of accident there the other day, too? I heard something about Logan finding you in the river."

"Something like that. He found me along the river's edge."

Why was he asking? Curiosity?

Will's mouth opened, as if to ask another question, but then he smiled. "I'm glad he could help you. How are you recovering?"

"I'm doing pretty well. I think I'll be avoiding the canyon for a while, though."

"Too bad. It's a beautiful place." Will's dark eyes lingered on her face, his lips curving into a grin that veered toward flirtatious. Maybe he was trying to be friendly, not pry.

Those files were messing with her head. Not every ranger was secretly helping Jimenez. She just needed to find the one who was.

"Yes, it is. How long have you been a ranger here, Will?"

"A couple of years, but my family is from Texas."

"Oh?" He looked Hispanic, with his dark hair and eyes, but she didn't want to make him feel like he was under interrogation. His file had included the background check they'd run when he was hired. Nothing of interest, except for one relative south of the border. A distant cousin. "Did you grow up nearby?"

"El Paso. My father was American, my mother Mexican." He winked. "It's okay, everybody wonders. They're just not brave enough to ask."

She smiled in a vain attempt to cover up her curiosity. "Sykes isn't exactly a Hispanic name. So…" She paused. "How do you like working here?"

"It's been…good." His focus shifted for a moment, as if he were thinking about other things. Almost as quickly, he turned his attention back to Ashley. Flashing her another one of those perfect, movie-star grins, he asked, "Are you planning on sticking around? I mean, after all the bad things that have happened?"

She smiled, but her brows pulled together in confusion. Did rangers quit right away that often? "I'm planning on it for now. Don't think they'd approve a transfer quite yet."

Was he happy or not about that answer?

And the Mexican cousin… Was there a connection?

He pulled away from the door. His gaze was cryptic as he glanced back. "You won't regret it."

Logan was on the verge of falling asleep at his desk.

Time to call it a night. The shadows had grown long and he craved a shower and a meal. He locked his office door and headed out across the parking lot toward his house, debating whether he should check on Ashley.

The memory of her wet hair lingered against his arm, the warmth of her body cradled against his chest. *No. Work. Keep it about work.* Maybe all the pain of Erin was long gone, but the memory of it wasn't. Those months after she'd left had been some of the hardest of his life.

So much joy followed by crushing despair. No way was he going to endure that kind of heartbreak again.

He'd made it worse for himself—always aware in the back of his mind that she *might* call. Might change her mind once she realized what she'd lost. He hadn't given up hope until his mom had told him Erin was engaged. The fact she'd told his family first had only twisted the knife in his back.

Still, that was years ago now. Once he'd come to terms with reality—with God's call to singleness and dedicating his life to protecting this corner of creation—he'd been happy.

He *was* happy. Or, he had been, until Ashley showed up.

But no matter what kind of havoc she wreaked on his emotions, she still needed his help. No harm in walking past her house to make sure everything appeared safe.

The lingering afternoon heat was fading away with the last embers of daylight, the first stars peeking through the veil of deepening twilight as he strode into the neighborhood behind headquarters. As he approached Ashley's house—the only one with lights on in her section of the street—he slowed. The door was ajar, someone standing in the doorway.

It looked like…Will Sykes. Well, wasn't that considerate of him? And such a coincidence, given that Ashley was both pretty and apparently unattached. Will sure wouldn't have showed up at any other ranger's house to check on them.

Not that it should matter to me. Ashley had made it clear she wanted to take care of herself.

Will left her house and she closed the door. Logan ducked behind a car on the street to avoid being seen, even though it was ridiculous. He should go home. Forget all about it. He had found out what he'd wanted to know. She was safe.

But his feet wouldn't comply. They carried him up to Ashley's door, where he knocked firmly.

"Just a minute!" Ashley called from inside.

After a moment she opened the door, her smile fading into surprise at the sight of him instead of Will. "Hi, Logan."

He stood on her doorstep, forgetting why he was there. She was stunning, thick chocolate hair hanging past her shoulders, the ends flipped into unruly curls.

"I…" He swallowed, striving for some semblance of professionalism. "I wanted to check on you. After what happened today." He stuffed his hands into his pockets. This woman had a knack for turning him back into an awkward teenager.

Even more embarrassing, she didn't look at all awkward. If anything, she looked annoyed, with her eyebrows raised and her lips pressed together. "I'm fine, Logan. Really." She stayed in the doorway, the door partially closed against her back. "If I need anything, I know where to find you."

An obvious dismissal. But he wasn't giving up that easily. "I'm sorry about earlier today."

"It wasn't your—"

He held up his hand. "Not the stream and the Jeep. I mean about thinking you were keeping information from me. If we're going to work together, we need to trust each other."

Her face paled. Or was it a trick of the light? "Not a big deal. Don't mention it."

"It has to be hard for you, having your memories erased and then trickling back bit by bit."

"It's been…unpleasant, to say the least." She gnawed

at her lip, her gaze focused on the ground. Her smile was back in place when she looked up again. "But I'm fine. Thanks for checking."

Was that confusion flickering in her dark eyes? He casually glanced past her, noting the open laptop on the coffee table illuminated by the lamp's glow. These old houses didn't have WiFi or cell phone reception. What was she working on in there? "Have you been able to get in touch with any of your family or friends?"

Her eyes widened a bit and she sucked in a slow breath before answering. "Um, no." She waved a hand vaguely toward the living room. "Maybe I could use the internet at headquarters?"

"Of course. I should've offered sooner." He smiled, trying to ignore the questions swirling in his brain. Why hadn't she asked? Wouldn't she want to tell her family she'd made it here safely, now that she'd remembered them? "In fact, why don't we walk over there now?"

Her mouth hung open for a fraction of a second before she clamped it into a smile. "Sure. Let me grab my computer." She wiped both hands against her jeans and retreated into the living room.

Sweaty palms, a sign of discomfort. Or was she lying? If only there was a way to check her pulse…

"Hey," he called after her, "before we walk over there, let me check your eyes for concussion symptoms again. I should've done that after we got back, but I didn't think about it."

She tilted her head to one side, one eyebrow quirked.

"Yes, it's necessary," he insisted. "Doctor's orders, remember?"

"Fine." The scowl lingered on her face as she stood before him, clutching the laptop.

Now, to get her to lie again, if that's what she'd been doing.

He slipped both hands around her jaw, making sure a couple of his fingers rested over the steady thump of her pulse. All of it to better examine her eyes, of course.

Such a beautiful color. Dark like coffee, wide and trusting.

Focus. He cleared his throat, tilting her head one way and then the other to watch the movement of her eyes. "I'm sure your parents will be relieved to hear from you. Do you want to email or call?"

"Email will be fine," she murmured. Her irises were fascinating, the way they had that ring of dark around the pupil, radiating into lighter, almost golden edges. Like honey.

Such a curious mix of strength and vulnerability rolled into one woman. He rubbed a thumb gently across her jawbone. Her pulse danced erratically beneath his last two fingers.

When she swallowed, her throat bobbed beneath his touch. "Am I okay?"

Logan blinked, whipping back his hands like he'd been caressing a rattlesnake. His heart hammered like it would pound its way out of his chest. "Absolutely. Great recovery. I think you're well on your way." He practically leaped to the sidewalk. "Let's go, before it gets late."

So much for that idea.

Ashley could scarcely get her lungs to draw in adequate oxygen as she closed the front door. Good thing holding the laptop hid her trembling hands. Granted, she was still missing a year's worth of memories, but to her recollection, she'd never been that close to a man before.

Not one that attracted her like a magnet, anyway.

She'd had boys who were friends. She'd gone on a couple of dates. But she'd been so absorbed with academics in school, and then with her career, she'd never invested much effort in romance. Somehow it had always felt like an either-or choice. She knew a handful of special agents who managed to balance both full-time work and family, but most of them were men. And throwing kids into the mix? No thanks. Her work was rigorous and demanding—why try to add more to an already full plate?

She'd always prioritized focusing on things she could control. Like becoming a federal agent.

And solving this case.

But no amount of evaluating the sidewalk would remove the warm strength of Logan's hands on her skin, or the way he'd studied her face. He'd been doing his job—that was all—and she needed to do likewise.

"Job. Focus on the job," she muttered.

"What?" he asked, a half step ahead of her.

"Huh?" Her cheeks warmed. "Nothing."

Good grief. Answering his questions about her family without outright lying had been hard enough. This attraction to him was unacceptable.

On the positive side, maybe a little communication with the outside world would be helpful. As long as her protocol for contacting Morton hadn't changed in the last year, maybe she could access any shared files or messages he'd sent in the past couple of days.

Logan held the door open for her when they reached headquarters. A handful of rangers and other staff members was still there, wrapping up the day's concerns.

"You'll get your own cubicle in there—" he pointed to a room crammed with gray-fabric-covered dividers "—as soon as we can clear out a space. For tonight, it'll be easier to use my office."

"Thanks." She smiled warmly, grateful for the added privacy.

It took a few minutes to connect her laptop to the park's internet service, but then Logan left her alone. After confirming the network's security, she pulled up the encryption program on her laptop and connected to the Bureau's messaging system, which, mercifully, worked exactly as she remembered.

A quick message to Morton informed him of her arrival and the damage to the rental car, but she was careful to downplay the incident as a random break-in. If he even suspected her cover had been blown, or that someone was after her, he'd pull her out before she could make the connections she so desperately needed.

A return email arrived almost instantly.

Contact wants to meet in San Vicente.
Thursday, 1:00 p.m. Behind the chapel.
He'll find you. Go alone.
Morton.

Alone... Ashley drummed her fingers on the desk. That meant Morton didn't suspect a double-cross and he was concerned she'd scare off their contact if she brought backup. Not to mention that whole issue of not knowing whom to trust.

Logan had mentioned San Vicente—it was one of the small towns across the border. How could she get there without drawing suspicion either from him or whoever knew she was here?

Maybe she could convince Logan to go with her and then separate herself for a few minutes. Long enough to find the chapel.

She'd have to give it some more thought, but one way

or another, she'd make this meet. For the first time in days, hope bubbled in her chest. Maybe she'd finally get some of the clues she needed to figure out how everything tied together.

NINE

Logan glanced up at the clock for the tenth time as he pulled a folder out of his desk. Ashley should be arriving for work any minute. He'd walked her home after she'd sent her emails last night, but he'd kept their interaction as professional as possible and she'd seemed happy to do likewise.

No more touching.

Ever.

She appeared in his office long before he felt ready.

"Hi, Logan." She sat in the chair across the desk. She was dressed once more in her ranger uniform, her hair tucked neatly back behind her head. Her expression was one of indifferent friendliness, like he could be any old person in the office. Not someone who'd been staring into her eyes the night before. Good—that should make it easier to rebuild the wall he had to keep between them.

"Good morning," he replied. "How did you sleep?"

"Well enough. Any news on the shooters at Santa Elena?"

He shook his head, hardly surprised it would be her first question. "Border patrol couldn't find any trace of them. The downpour didn't help. We could send men across the border, but the odds of them finding anything…"

"Wouldn't be very good," she finished for him. "So much for that idea."

"With no evidence of drug running, or anyone crossing the border, we're calling it a random act of violence. Maybe even gang-related. You and I were in the wrong place at the wrong time."

"Is that what *you* think?" She raised an eyebrow, her gaze intent.

Fishing for the answer she wanted. *Tough.* He wasn't a rookie and he had to play by the rules. He shrugged. "We have nothing to go on, no evidence besides that map you won't share with anyone else, so at this point, officially, I have to agree with the chief ranger."

"And unofficially?"

"Until you can remember more, I'm not sure it matters what I think. Not much we can do, other than monitor the situation."

"There hasn't been any organized crime here we might link the shootings with?"

"Nothing beyond what we talked about yesterday. I don't know what kind of skeletons you're looking for, but we've got a pretty clean closet here. Other than a few petty crimes, the biggest dangers around here are from the landscape and the wildlife. Not people."

"Of course." She flashed a small, tight-lipped smile straight from the Mona Lisa.

Did she not believe him? Either that or, back to Logan's original suspicion: she was keeping secrets. Just like the Mona Lisa. "What?"

She shook her head and stared at the poster of native Big Bend plants on the wall behind him. From the unfocused look in her eyes, she was lost in thought.

"For your training today—" he began finally.

But she cut him off, as if she hadn't even heard him speak. "We should look for the mine."

"We should do what?" He raised his eyebrows.

Her eyes snapped to his, alert once more. "There's a reason someone sent me that map. Maybe the only way to find out why is to locate the mine."

"You do realize we were almost killed yesterday, don't you?"

"Obviously. But since you agree that yesterday's incident was a random occurrence, what's your objection?"

He ran his hand through his hair. Difficult woman. "Ashley, you clearly haven't told me everything you know. And even this map—you refuse to take it to the chief ranger. Your house and your car have both been broken into. Somebody wants something from you, and the facts aren't adding up. What are you not telling me?"

"I don't expect you to understand." She shrugged. "I've told you as much as I can. If you want me to spend the day on training exercises, fine. I can take care of this in my free time."

"Right." He couldn't hold back a snort. "As if I would let you go traipsing out into the Chisos alone after all the things that have already happened to you."

He held her gaze for a long moment, her dark eyes stubbornly refusing to yield. She lifted her chin, as if to crush any hope she might change her mind.

Nothing for it. "Fine." Why was he was agreeing to this mad scheme? "But I'm coming with you."

"Deal." Ashley's grin lit up the room.

Seeing her smile made the whole madcap plan worth it. "Where do we start?"

She spread the tattered map out on the desk between them, puzzling over the writing. "For how meticulously the map was drawn, whoever made it could've written a little bit neater."

"Rather particular about your treasure maps, aren't you?"

Her lips tipped, laughter dancing at the corner of her eyes, and she pointed at an arrow drawn from the Mexican town of San Vicente across the border toward the Chisos. There was a large chunk of Spanish text beside it. "Do you have that Spanish-English dictionary?"

He nodded, pulling it off one of the shelves behind his desk. A cascade of papers fluttered to the floor. Filling out paperwork was *not* one of his strengths. He handed Ashley the book and stooped to gather the loose forms.

"You have heard of filing cabinets, haven't you?" she asked. "Or is this park too remote?"

"Ha, ha, very funny." Logan shoved the messy stack back onto the shelf. "I may not be organized, but I have other virtues."

She flashed him another grin before turning her attention to the task of translating. He watched her work, so efficient and focused. Somehow, she managed to look as at home in her ranger uniform as she had in that fancy business suit the first day he'd met her.

After a moment she smiled again, this time without looking up. "You can quit watching me do all the work, you know."

He shrugged. "There's nothing else for me to do at the moment." Besides, it was fascinating the way that one clump of hair kept coming loose from behind her ear, no matter how many times she tucked it back.

"Here's what I've got. 'Chapel steps at dawn on Easter morning—first light touches the entrance.'" She glanced up. "Can you even see the Chisos Mountains from San Vicente?"

He pulled out a current park map, laying it beside the hand-drawn one. "Chilicotal Mountain lies between San Vicente and the Chisos, but it's a good 3,000 feet shorter, so you can still see the peaks from the river."

"Time for a day trip?" That speculative gleam in her eye suggested she wasn't going to take *no* for an answer.

"We could go—" he shrugged "—but we're about six months too early for Easter morning."

She held up a finger, shaking it as she spoke. "But what really matters is where the sun would have first hit the peak five hundred years ago, when the Spanish first found it."

Logan picked up her train of thought. "So, if we photograph the mountain peak, maybe with a little research we can extrapolate where the entrance should be?"

"Exactly."

"*If* this mine even exists."

"Of course." Her smile was obviously fake. Agreeing for the sake of keeping the peace. "How about Thursday? Since we have that staff picnic this afternoon."

When he'd told her about it earlier, she'd practically grimaced. She didn't exactly strike him as the social type. "Remembered, did you? I'm impressed."

Ashley handed him the dictionary, her face scrunching. "Yeah, about that…do I have to go?"

Ah, right. Trying to get out of it, after all. But he could be stubborn, too. "You'll get to meet more of the other rangers." He folded the park map. "Besides, a little fun will be good for you."

Ashley sent a quick confirmation message to Morton and left work early under the pretense of needing time to get ready. In reality, it would only take five minutes to change out of her park uniform, but Logan didn't argue.

After how easy it had been to convince him to take her to San Vicente, she could hardly complain about being dragged to a picnic.

As soon as she walked into the house, she dropped her keys on the coffee table and pulled out her laptop. It had occurred to her that maybe she'd find files on some of the other rangers on her computer. Useful information prior to meeting more of them in person.

Sure enough, she had personnel files from the Department of the Interior—she had no idea how Morton had gotten them without going through Barclay and arousing suspicion—and perhaps, better yet, personal information gathered through the Bureau's resources.

Her hand hovered over the computer mouse. The list was alphabetical, containing almost a hundred files. But one name immediately drew her attention and, unable to resist, she clicked on the file marked *Logan Everett*. He had become her partner, so she needed to know whether he was trustworthy. But logic couldn't shake the guilt niggling at her conscience as she read his file.

Thirty-two years old—about what she'd guessed. Graduated with honors from a top environmental science program before going directly into the park service. Three years at Crater Lake—that must've been beautiful—and now seven years here. He'd taken on the role of training new rangers about four years ago.

She moved on to his personal information, shifting in her seat and wishing she had the luxury of waiting for him to tell her all these facts when he was ready. But everything she read was, if anything, admirable. Newspaper clippings showed various things he'd done during his time with the park service: a few criminal arrests, but mostly successful search-and-rescue operations.

Exactly the sort of man you'd want on your side for an investigation. And no motive to help Rico Jimenez.

She moved on to others she'd already met: Ed Chambers, Will Sykes, the superintendent. Ed had a sick sister who needed surgery. The superintendent had recently gone through a divorce. His only daughter was in college. Will had only been with the park service for two years—Big Bend was his first assignment. His father had died a long time ago, leaving his mother to raise him and his sister alone. They still lived in a suburb of El Paso.

Reading the files was like sifting through everyone's laundry, searching for the stinky socks.

And still more than ninety files to go. Ashley shut the computer, momentarily disgusted with her job. Was this hunt a waste of her time? Maybe Jimenez was a criminal genius and didn't need anybody's help. Maybe there weren't any dirty socks to find. The thought that any of these people—so dedicated, so willing to make sacrifices to protect others—could be a traitor, made her stomach churn.

She just hoped—no, *prayed*—that that someone wasn't Logan, because sometimes it was the person you'd never suspect.

It took less than five minutes to change into the only dress she'd brought with her and to run a comb through her hair. Then she slipped her laptop into its hiding place under the mattress and tucked the map into the camisole she wore underneath her dress.

"Hey, Ashley." Will sauntered toward her as she approached the party, carrying a drink in his hand. His crisp, white shirt matched his perfect teeth and contrasted beautifully with his dark skin and hair. "I was hoping you'd be here."

She smiled ruefully. "Logan told me I had to come."

"I'm glad he did." To her surprise, Will took her arm, leading her toward the crowded tent. As they walked, she caught a sudden scent on the breeze—something clean, like detergent or fabric softener. Strikingly familiar but gone before she could place it.

There probably weren't more than a hundred residents in Panther Junction, but it appeared that most of them had made it to this event. And now they were watching her walk arm-in-arm with Will Sykes, jumping to who-knew-what conclusions. Ashley extricated her arm under the pretense of smoothing some flyaway hairs from her face. They all knew Will—they would know he was merely being friendly.

And he proved to be a great escort. Not only did he seem to be on good terms with everyone, he made a point to introduce her. She soon lost track—elementary school teachers, interpretive rangers, postal clerks, the janitorial staff. Most of them looked about a thousand times more likely to win a quilting bee or a game of shuffleboard than to secretly help a Mexican drug lord. Still, she would check their files later.

The small talk was already wearing on her by the time Ed Chambers clattered a wooden spoon against one of the tables. "Welcome, everyone," he called. After offering a short prayer, he invited all of them to line up and "dig in" to the heaping platters of beef brisket, potato salad and beans.

She took her loaded plate and followed Will to a table, mentally cataloguing each new person she met. And *not* looking around the crowd for Logan.

He came up to her as she threw away her trash. "Well?" A mischievous light glinted in his eyes.

"Well what?" Despite the heat creeping into her cheeks at his nearness, she held his steady gaze.

"Did you get the meat sweats?"

"Excuse me?" She did her best to look politely disgusted.

He laughed. "You know, when you eat too much meat."

"Ugh. You don't need to say anything else."

"That's my girl. I knew you would like the brisket." He put his arm around her shoulders and squeezed, unknowingly setting off an electric jolt through her insides.

What on earth was *wrong* with her? She was a federal agent, not a high-schooler.

"Ashley—" Will walked up to them "—want an escort home? Unless you need to stay longer?" The half smirk on his face as he glanced at Logan's hand on her shoulder filled her cheeks with heat.

She pulled away, swallowing her embarrassment. Logan was her trainer, after all. There was *nothing* personal.

"No, go ahead." Logan stuffed his hands into his pockets. "I'll see you in the morning."

"So, want to talk about it?" Ed Chambers asked as they walked over to park headquarters.

Logan stopped wiping at the barbecue sauce hopelessly smeared across his shirt and glanced up at his friend. "What?" he snapped, instantly regretting his tone of voice. It wasn't Ed's fault Logan had plowed into the trash can.

No, come to think of it, maybe it *was* Ed's fault. He had paired Logan and Ashley together, after all. And if Logan had been watching where he was going instead of staring at her brown hair dancing in the breeze…

Ed glanced over his shoulder, toward the tent. "Whatever, or whoever, was distracting you back there. I have a guess already."

"Maybe it's none of your business, old man." He couldn't hold back a laugh. Ed had been both a friend and spiritual mentor to him for years—there could be no keeping secrets from him.

They reached headquarters and Ed unlocked the door, pulling it open. "I'm glad to see you're finally opening yourself up to new possibilities. She's the first woman to turn your head in a long time."

"Who said it had anything to do with her?"

Ed raised his hands in mock surrender. "Just making an observation. I'll see you later."

"Hey, Ed?" Logan called as the chief ranger turned to go. "What else do you know about Ashley? Why is she here?"

A curious expression flickered on Ed's face but vanished almost immediately. He shrugged. "Providence, I guess. Why?"

Did he know more than he was saying? Logan opened his office door. "I'm concerned about her."

"That's why I picked you to train her."

After saying good-night to Ed, Logan pored over the park map on his desk. If only he could feel so confident. Personal feelings aside, he still worried about Ashley. They'd left Santa Elena Canyon alive only by the grace of God. What if someone *was* after that map? How was he going to keep her safe the next time? She was quite capable with the law-enforcement side, but she didn't know the terrain like he did. And after what had happened with Sam...

He wanted to believe what Superintendent Barclay thought—that the shooting had been a random incident.

Bored teenagers daring each other. Or maybe the newest cartel member proving his loyalty by taking shots across the border.

But deep down, he didn't believe it. Of course, that left an even bigger question. How had anyone known Ashley would be there? Or were they waiting, in case she came back?

And what had happened to her that first night, when he had found her near the river?

Too many questions without any answers. And the woman herself working against him. One minute she would be in his arms, staring up at him with those eyes large enough for a man to drown in, and the next she was pushing him away. Refusing his help. Keeping her secrets.

He pursed his lips together. Ed was right—he *hadn't* felt this way about anyone since Erin.

That thought was almost more terrifying than anything else.

TEN

Ashley kept her hand tucked into her pocket to keep from glancing at her watch. The steeple of the San Vicente chapel stretched its small brown cross up to the brilliant blue sky on the far side of the marketplace, beckoning her as she wound her way between the vendors' booths. From their position on the northwest corner, the steps should have a perfect view of the US side of the river.

The small square was a feast for the senses, packed with colors and textures and spicy, pungent smells. Along the edges of the square, sand-colored adobe buildings stood sentry, their bright awnings flapping in the breeze.

Fifteen minutes. She had fifteen minutes to stroll through this marketplace, find a way to ditch Logan at the last second and identify her contact at the chapel. Would he or she be waiting in the street behind it?

At least they were dressed like tourists. Logan carried a Nikon DSLR slung in a bag across his broad shoulders, ready to snap pictures from the chapel steps. The perfect pretense for being there, but she hoped he wouldn't scare her contact away.

She paused in front of a booth full of blankets, fingering the vibrantly woven wool. The vendor smiled, his brown face crinkling around his dark eyes. Hoping for a sale, no doubt.

"Can we shop later?" Logan stopped next to her and nudged her with his elbow. He'd stayed on her heels like a loyal dog—she laughed at the image, pretty sure he wouldn't find it quite as funny. The way he kept scanning the square, as if he assumed somebody was about to jump them at any second, was sure to chase off her contact at this rate. Logan didn't have FBI training, of course, but it'd be nice if he could be a *little* more covert about it.

One of these blankets *would* make a lovely gift for her parents...

"You know—" she smiled sweetly up at him "—my mom's birthday is coming up. She'd love one of these blankets. Why don't you go ahead?" She nodded toward the chapel. "I'll catch up in a minute."

His brows pulled together into a slight frown. "For somebody so insistent on coming down here, I don't get how you could shop at a time like this."

She shrugged. "The chapel's not going anywhere. Five minutes won't kill me."

He raised a brow, his lips pursing to one side. "Women and shopping."

A decidedly false stereotype, in Ashley's case—she'd far rather be at the shooting range—but she could hardly say that to Logan, so she shrugged again and waved him off toward the chapel. "Five minutes."

He hesitated, scanning the market again.

"I'll be fine." She looked at him pointedly.

"All right." He let out a resigned sigh, evidently deciding he wasn't going to win this argument, and ambled off toward the chapel.

One problem solved. Ashley snuck a glance at her watch. Less than ten minutes. She picked up one of the blankets, barely paying attention to the intricate black, green and white weaving, and purchased it from the vendor without haggling.

His wide grin assured her she'd probably paid more than anybody else in the market would've, but she could chalk it up to keeping up her disguise as a tourist. Stupid Americans, right?

In the distance, Logan glanced back at her and waved. She held up the blanket, pasting on a ridiculous smile of delight at her new treasure.

As soon as his back was turned, she tucked the blanket under one arm and slowly wove her way toward the chapel, doing her best to look like she was following Logan but veering a little more to the left. When he disappeared around the front of the chapel, she cut straight across the square, ducking around textile booths and stepping past carts laden with tomatoes, peppers and corn.

She'd almost reached the far side of the square when a man stepped in front of her, holding a tray of silver jewelry.

"Pretty lady," he said in broken English. "See the jewelry?" His face was wrinkled and weathered, and his smile revealed a chipped front tooth.

On the far side of his booth, an alley led behind the old chapel. The bright overhead sun cast a heavy shadow along the chapel's back wall, but nobody appeared to be waiting for her. Farther down, the alley was empty, save for laundry hanging on lines strung between the houses. Maybe her contact wasn't here yet. She still had five minutes or so.

The man pushed the tray at her. "Lovely, yes?"

"Yes." She scanned the booths around her. Nothing out of the ordinary. And, thankfully, no sign of Logan.

"Come, see more." The man set his tray down on his stand, beckoning her closer.

Might as well. She could keep a good eye on the alley from here and, in a couple of minutes, she'd cut between this booth and the neighbor selling baskets and slip into the alley to wait.

Some of the pieces were quite lovely. Beautiful craftsmanship.

"Did you make—?" she started to ask, but the man placed a rough hand on her arm and tipped his head toward the alley. Her contact?

"This way," he whispered.

Nobody seemed interested as she followed the man behind the booth, ducking with him into the dark shadows beside the crumbling adobe wall of the chapel. They both glanced up and down the alley to make sure no one lurked nearby. Empty. Above them, the chapel's large cast-iron bell gonged once to mark the hour.

"Agent Thompson?" The man kept his voice low. He gazed over her shoulder, toward the marketplace and his unattended booth.

Ashley nodded. She'd followed him into the alley. If this was a setup, the cat was already out of the proverbial bag. "What do you have for me?"

"Jimenez knows you go undercover in park."

She clenched her teeth, fighting the unease knotting her stomach. *Not* what she was hoping to hear. "How?"

He shook his head. "I do not know."

Cover blown. Should she call Morton, abandon the mission? She'd suspected as much after the break-in at her house, but with this confirmation…

No. She was here for a reason, beyond catching Jimenez, and she was determined to figure out what it was. The street was still empty. She fished out the map, which she'd stowed along with her passport inside a plastic sandwich bag in a pouch beneath her waistband. She showed it to the man, indicating the mine. "Do you know where this is?"

His eyes widened slightly. "Is where Jimenez gets gold. Pine Canyon Trail." He pointed to a long squiggly line running below the mine, and then dragged his finger down to another set of mountains closer to the border. "Drives gold out from Juniper Canyon to hide it here, until he can cross border."

She'd ask Logan the names of those mountains next chance she got. The illegal mining alone would be enough to arrest Jimenez, but knowing the way the cartel lords operated, he was bound to have other infractions. Illegal laborers. Weapons. Drugs. They'd put him away for a long time, *if* she could catch him before he got to her. "Thank you. Where is he now? At the mine?"

"Goes back and forth." The man waggled his finger between the mine and the southern mountains. "Work during day. Drive out gold at night."

It was enough. Ashley's heart soared inside her chest. With a little surveillance, they'd catch him. Maybe she'd finally figure out why this place mattered.

She folded the map, sealed it back inside its plastic bag—just in case—and tucked the pouch beneath her waistband. She touched the man's arm. "Thank you. We'll see he gets the justice he deserves."

The man nodded, his lips pressed into a thin line, eyes turning liquid. "For my Lena." He swallowed, blinked a few times, and walked past Ashley back to his booth.

She lingered in the shadows a moment longer, scanning the marketplace for Logan's tall figure, but finding no sign of him. The crowd had thinned now that it was afternoon. The heat scorched the dusty, packed earth of the square. She edged along the chapel wall, following it behind vendors' booths, as she kept an eye on the marketplace.

Something felt off—she didn't know what, but her instincts told her to stay alert.

A moment later she spied two men hurrying through the booths. One was white, the other Mexican. Both were muscular and wore cargo pants, white shirts and heavy utility belts. They ignored the goods and produce, and instead surveyed the shoppers, their dark eyes drifting periodically to the narrow alleys providing access to the square. Almost as if they were looking for someone.

The hairs stood on the back of her neck. She glanced back at the man from the jewelry booth. His stand was nearly empty as he hastily wrapped up the last of the necklaces and rings on display.

Ashley hurried along the chapel wall, trying to keep the nearby booths and their occupants between her and the two men. They still scanned the square, but they'd picked up their pace.

She rounded the front corner of the chapel, letting out a quick burst of breath at the sight of Logan standing on the chapel steps, blissfully unaware of the men on her tail. He held the camera up to his eye, taking a series of shots of the landscape across the river.

Here the terrain dropped down from the plateau, giving an unobstructed view above the rooftops of the small San Vicente homes built onto the hillside. Down near the glittering ribbon of the Rio Grande stood the old 1775 presidio, a large, square-ish adobe structure used as a fort by the Spanish. On the far side, vast desert stretched up to the roots of the Chisos, jutting like ragged teeth from the surrounding flatland.

"Logan." She tugged on his sleeve. "We need to go."

He lowered the camera, his face crinkling in annoyance. "You messed up my shot." His green eyes drifted over the blanket still tucked under her arm. "Glad you found what you wanted."

Ashley released his sleeve and took a step back, peering out into the square. Her breath caught.

The men were gone.

Logan tucked the camera into the bag dangling at his side. He'd gotten some good shots. Hard to say how helpful they'd be, though. He glanced at Ashley, wrinkling his forehead. He'd never understand women. She'd been so determined to come here, and now she couldn't stop staring at the marketplace. He hardly would've pegged her for the shop-till-you-drop type.

"They're gone," she said, the blood draining from her face.

His hand automatically dropped to his waistband before he remembered there was no gun. Mexican law only allowed select US agents to bear arms, and only with special written permission from the government. Big Bend park rangers didn't make the cut. "Who?"

"The men in the market. Come on." The words tumbled out of her mouth as she grabbed his arm, tugging him around the far side of the chapel, away from the square. The dirt road was narrow and dark, lined with tightly packed adobe homes. Ashley let go of his arm and jogged along the side, keeping close to the chapel wall.

Logan followed, glancing behind them as they went, but the alley remained empty. "What men? Where are we going?"

She paused at the back of the chapel and peered around the corner into the cross street. "Two men in the marketplace. I think they were following me."

He peered over her shoulder, the strawberry scent of her hair filling his nose. The street was empty. "Maybe we can lose them between here and the other side of town."

"We'll have to catch a ride to the border crossing." Her pretty face held an uncharacteristic grimace. "There's no way to walk back without being seen."

They'd left the park at the official border crossing at Boquillas, paying ten bucks to a teenage boy to row them across the river. The only way to cross the six or so miles from Boquillas to San Vicente was in the bed of a pickup, and they'd need the same way back. "We'll figure something out," he promised. "If we can slip out of town unnoticed, we'll be okay."

They darted across the street, keeping close to the buildings and the little bit of shadow created by the midday sun. Noise from the lingering crowd in the market carried down the alley. A low, rhythmic sound echoed below the murmur of the crowd.

Footsteps. And close.

He stopped, snatching Ashley's shirtsleeve, and they both pressed back against a dusty wall coated in chipping orange plaster.

Two men turned into the alley from behind the chapel. Both stocky and muscular, and no doubt carrying at least one illegal firearm apiece. One of them pointed at Logan and Ashley. *"¡Por ahí!"*

"Run." Logan gave her a little shove, but she was already off, sprinting down the narrow street.

He followed as they took one turn after another, dodging children playing ball and hapless burros led by scrunched old men. South around the marketplace, then west, zigzagging up and down the narrow streets, heading ever closer to the road that would lead them out of San Vicente.

She pulled up after a few minutes and Logan glanced behind them. No sign of their pursuers.

"Do you think we lost them?" She massaged a stitch in her side.

"Hope so. We're about out of real estate." He nodded toward the far end of the street, where the last little gaily painted cantina fended off the endless desert, its sign advertising cold *cervezas* creaking against a rusty frame. "Maybe we can catch a ride."

"Worth a try."

They jogged the last hundred yards to the small terrace surrounding the cantina. Benches lined both sides of its open door, covered by a bright yellow-and-orange awning to provide a welcome bit of shade. The couple of metal tables and chairs beneath the awning were empty.

Logan peered through the windows as they approached, then stuck his head inside the door, glancing both ways before giving Ashley the all-clear. A pair of old men sat at a table beneath the only ceiling fan, its rickety thumping blades scarcely making a dent in the oppressive heat.

A long, wooden counter occupied most of the small place, lined with tall metal stools. Shelves hung on the wall in the background and held an assortment of glassware and dingy framed photographs of tourists. A door at the end presumably led into the kitchen.

Ashley wiped her arm against her forehead and walked up to the bar. *"¡Hola!"* she called. When nobody answered, she glanced at Logan and shrugged. "That's about the extent of my Spanish."

His wasn't much better, but living in the park for a few

years had helped. He pulled out a handful of dollar bills and smacked the counter. *"Dos agua sin gas, por favor."*

A moment later an older man came out, wiping his hands on a white apron. *"Buenos días.* Hello. Americans. So nice. You want water?"

"Yes. Two bottles." Logan slid the money across the counter as the man slapped two tepid bottles down.

Ashley cracked hers open and guzzled it.

"Impressive." Logan winked, laughing when she blushed. He turned back to the man behind the counter. "We need a ride back to Boquillas. Can you help?"

The man eyed them for a moment, then nodded. "One moment. I see." The kitchen door swung shut behind him as he disappeared.

Logan leaned against the counter and slipped his hands into his pockets. No sign of their pursuers outside. The two old men sat at their table, languidly sipping bottles of beer and gesticulating with their hands.

Ashley perched on one of the stools, every one of her muscles taut like a coil ready to spring. Her dark hair, normally slicked back straight in a ponytail, fell in frizzy clumps around her cheeks. It was strange how calm she was, considering they were unarmed and under pursuit in a foreign country.

She was a constant mystery—one moment looking entirely out of place, the next like she belonged there. Erin had been the same in many ways, though never so coolly confident. Yet he'd still been blindsided when she told him she'd always hated Big Bend.

Ashley didn't seem to hate it, but maybe today would change her mind.

The door to the kitchen swung open and the man thumped back out, waving his hand for them to follow. "This way. My nephew give you ride. Fifteen dollar."

Logan let out a sigh of relief, exchanging a quick glance with Ashley. Her lips tilted into a half smile, her shoulders relaxing a touch. Maybe they'd get out without any more trouble, after all.

He and Ashley followed the man out beneath the awning and around to the back of the cantina. A lone bench with faded blue paint stood beside a dusty vending machine that had seen better days. Farther down, the cantina's wall disappeared into shadow beneath a makeshift roof of corrugated plastic, creating a storage shed between the cantina and the next building. The rusty bumper of a truck peeked out from the shadows.

The man pointed at the bench. "You wait. He be here in few minutes."

"Gracias," Logan said.

"De nada." The man disappeared around to the front, leaving them alone in the hundred-degree heat.

Ashley wiped sweat from her forehead and pointed at the truck. "Think that's our ride?"

"Maybe." He swallowed a few sips of warm water. "If it gets us to the border, that's what matters." The intense afternoon heat tugged a yawn out of his chest.

"I wish I could've gotten a better look at them." She gnawed on her lower lip, staring north across the desert.

"Do you think they were after…" He trailed off, not wanting to mention the map out loud. Just in case.

She nodded. "Maybe the same ones who tried to break into my house."

"We'll run the descriptions through the database when we get back. Maybe it'll turn up a hit." He patted the camera bag. "At least I got the shots before we had to run."

"That's something." She paced back and forth in front of the vending machine, glancing alternately between the desert and her wristwatch. "Has it been a few minutes yet?"

The truck engine in the shed sputtered to life. Logan went rigid, stepping between Ashley and the vehicle more out of habit than anything else. But he relaxed as it eased out from under the awning, rolling toward them.

"Sí, señorita."

Logan and Ashley both spun at the voice coming from the corner of the cantina.

One of the men who'd been chasing them stood there, his gun aimed at Ashley's head.

Logan raised his hands slowly, nudging Ashley's arm when she hesitated. His mind raced through their options, coming up dismally short beyond priority number one. Not getting shot. "We don't want any trouble. Tourists."

"Right." The man smirked. "Then we have a tour all lined up for you." He was white, perhaps an inch over six feet tall, two hundred pounds, American accent. Hair color possibly light brown, but hard to say under the blue ball cap.

The truck stopped, its engine idling. The other man, Mexican, with a long, jagged scar cutting across his right cheek, sat behind the wheel. He tapped the glass behind his seat and a third man, whom Logan hadn't seen before, hopped out of the bed of the truck.

Also armed.

Ashley stiffened.

First rule of an abduction was to stay out of the vehicle. But with two guns trained on their heads, they hardly had a choice.

"Into the truck," the American ordered.

"Where are you taking us?" Ashley asked.

He angled the muzzle of his gun up over her shoulder and fired, the bullet lodging into the cantina's yellow plaster wall a few feet beyond her. Logan shot her a warning glance, his stomach clenching into knots. Her face was pale, but her knees didn't wobble. The woman had nerves of steel.

Something cold and hard pressed against the back of his skull—the other gun. He gritted his teeth.

Ashley's eyes went wide with alarm. If all they wanted was the map, or something else she had, maybe he was disposable.

The American nodded.

Time slowed, each millisecond passing in an eternal haze of waiting for the click of the trigger, the impact of the bullet, the loss of consciousness. The moment he'd see Jesus face to face, after the blinding agony of death.

"No!" Fear laced Ashley's voice, tugging at his heart.

The impact came, but not the click. And the bullet felt heavier, blunter, more crushing than he'd expected. He crumpled to the ground, stars flaring in the blackness.

The last thing he heard was the American's voice, repeating his order to Ashley. "Get in the truck."

ELEVEN

Ashley couldn't see where they were going as the truck jostled and bounced over the uneven dirt road, but at least they were both still alive. She'd thought, for a moment there, they'd kill Logan. When the man had hit him with the butt of his gun instead, her legs had gone so weak she'd nearly collapsed.

His breathing was slow and steady, his eyes still closed, as he lay facing her on the hot metal of the truck bed. Ropes chafed at her ankles and wrists, bound behind her back, and the smell of exhaust choked her.

Logan stirred as the truck slowed to a stop.

"Logan?" she whispered.

He blinked a few times, his gaze snapping into focus when he saw her face. The back gate dropped open with a loud clang. Somebody barked rapid commands in Spanish and the man who'd ridden in the back with them, his gun always aimed at her chest, yanked on the ropes around her ankles.

She sat up, scooching herself toward the tailgate as the man pulled and stealing a quick glance at their surroundings. They were parked in the open courtyard of a large, square adobe structure—inside the presidio, she guessed. The walls were half in ruins, but a long, low building ran along the south side, close to where the truck was parked. Four or five open doorways suggested multiple rooms.

Beyond the walls, a little town—she assumed it was San Vicente—sat on a low hill a mile or two away. In the other direction lay the river, the Chisos Mountains and the United States.

Freedom.

But first they had to get out.

The men hauled her and Logan through one of the open doorways into a long room. Four high, narrow windows revealed glimpses of blue sky in the wall with the door. Heavy wood lintels stood above the door and windows, and hewed logs supported the roof. An empty niche in the back wall probably held a religious statue long ago. The only other items in the room were a single chair and a stack of decaying baskets.

"Tie them up." The order came from the man with the American accent. Working with a drug cartel to get rich. Ashley couldn't stop her nose from wrinkling in disgust. If she could figure out who he was, would that help her identify the insider with the park service?

She wanted to ask questions but decided to keep her mouth shut for the moment. They tied her to the room's lone chair and dragged Logan over to the end wall, looping his tied wrists over a hook above his head. Keeping him alive, thankfully. But why? Jimenez would never let either of them leave alive.

The answer, she knew, lay hidden inside the secret pouch, where she'd stowed the map after meeting her contact. Once they had it, she and Logan were as good as dead.

"Good." The American gestured to the man who'd driven the truck. "Manuel, report to the boss."

Jimenez. Did that mean he was here? Or were they merely calling him?

Across the room, Logan's head drooped and he groaned as he lifted it again. His shoulder blades jutted out in what had to be a terribly uncomfortable position.

Ashley's heart thrummed against her ribs. She had to get them out of here. Logan hadn't deserved to be dragged into this mess.

Focus. She needed to focus. Assess the situation, like she'd been trained. She flexed her hands behind her back. The ropes dug into her skin. No gun tucked comfortably under her waistband. Their best odds would be to get the two men out of the room. Give them a chance to figure out a plan.

The American bent in front of her, his face filling her vision. "Where is it?"

Ashley clamped her mouth shut.

"What…are you…talking about?" Logan sounded as if he was talking through a mouthful of packing peanuts. His eyes were still unfocused and dried blood was smeared across his cheek.

"Nobody asked you anything." The other man, the one who'd knocked him out, slapped him hard across the face. Ashley's stomach lurched at the sound.

Logan glared, spitting blood onto the floor. "What do you want from us?"

"The map, my friend. Where is it? Get your girlfriend to tell me and we will give you a painless death."

No less than she'd expected. They hadn't mentioned her contact, but they'd known she would be in San Vicente. Had he given her up or had it been somebody else? And if it was her contact, why give her all that information first? Was it false?

"Dunno what you're talking about," Logan mumbled.

The American ignored him, kneeling in front of Ashley, his face inches away. "Where is the map?" His fingers stopped inches away from her shirt. "Or shall I search for it myself?"

"Don't you dare touch her," Logan snarled, his tone fierce.

Ashley held the man's steely gaze, despite the fear skittering along her spine. She *hated* feeling vulnerable. Hearing about attacks on girls was one reason she'd chosen law enforcement in the first place.

His hand was very close.

She whipped her head forward, clamping her teeth down on his fingers as hard as she could. He howled, jerking back so fast he nearly pulled some of her teeth out.

His face turned splotchy red but when he finally spoke to her again, the words were calm. "Either you can tell me or we can do this the hard way."

When Ashley merely stared at him, unflinching, he nodded. "José."

The man called José drew back his fist and slammed it into Logan's unprotected stomach. A groan slipped out and his face contorted in agony.

Ashley pressed her lips together.

José struck again. And again—until the horrible muffled thump of each strike etched itself permanently into her mind.

That's why they'd kept him alive. To torture the truth out of her.

Her insides curdled with fear but she took a steadying breath. "Let him go. He doesn't know anything."

"No, no." The American contorted his mouth into a wicked grin. "You see, I don't like to hit women, so it's very convenient you brought him with you. Now, tell me where it is."

She couldn't look at Logan, not when he was paying for her silence. She shook her head.

The man didn't take his dark eyes off her face. "Again."

The impact was different this time—harder—bone on bone. When she dared a glance out of the corner of her eye, she could see blood trickling down the side of Logan's face. His eyes were steely, but how much could he take? Was the map worth Logan's life?

"I have been reasonable." The man rose to his feet. "This is your last chance. Tell me what I want to know." With a slow scraping sound, he drew a long knife from a sheath at his waist. He tapped it lazily against his outstretched palm.

That knife was coming for both of them, unless she thought of something quick.

Ashley ignored the shiver that crept up her spine. Time to take a gamble. "Why does Jimenez need it, anyway? We all know that mine is a legend."

Surprise flickered across Logan's features. And an unmistakable warning lit his eyes. *Tread carefully.*

The American laughed. "Because he likes to tie up loose ends. The last thing we need is the park service intruding into our business."

"How do you know they don't already have it?"

He didn't appear concerned as he paced back and forth in front of Ashley. "We have our ways. And once we have your copy and you both are gone, there will be no one else to stop us. Now, where is it?"

"Why should I tell you, if you're going to kill us anyway?"

Faster than she could blink, the man turned toward

Logan and released the knife. Ashley's heart lurched into her throat, stopping her breath, as the knife embedded itself into the adobe wall six inches from Logan's ear.

Slowly, carefully, the man walked over and pulled the knife out of the wall, tracing the blade along Logan's cheek. "Unless you want to watch me cut him apart, piece by piece, you will tell me what I want to know."

"Ashley," Logan growled, "don't listen to him. Don't worry about me."

The man laughed, kneeling in front of Ashley again, but safely beyond the reach of her teeth. He dropped his voice low, smirking. "He's brave, isn't he? But you know better. You know I will do it. And you are a woman— too weak to watch me carve him apart."

Oh, he would pay one day—when she brought down Jimenez and his men. But the red-hot anger flaring in her gut wasn't going to help now.

So instead she sighed deeply, hanging her head. "I'm sorry, Logan. I have to tell him. I couldn't bear…" She sniffled for effect.

The man stared at her, waiting expectantly.

What would he believe? A lie mixed with truth would be easiest to swallow. And whatever she said, she needed to get both men out of the room. "A man threatened me in the marketplace today. After that, I was scared, so I hid the map. You chased us before I could go back for it."

"Where? Here, in San Vicente?"

"The side street to the right of the chapel, off the plaza," Ashley said, infusing her voice with the weakness he expected to hear. "There was a crack in the adobe wall of the house across the street from the chapel's side entrance. I stuffed it in there, as high up as I could reach."

The man's eyes narrowed as he searched her face. He turned to his companion. "José, go get it."

José mumbled something in Spanish that Ashley didn't understand.

The other man frowned impatiently. "Fine. Wait outside. I don't want you killing them before I find the map."

He grabbed a fistful of Ashley's hair to expose her neck. With a sudden flick of his wrist, the long knife was at her throat. "If I find you've lied to me, you'll regret it."

She didn't dare breathe. The cold steel pricked unforgivingly at her skin. For a split second she thought he might kill her, but he pulled the knife away, releasing her hair. She slumped, tension ebbing out of her shoulders as the men stalked out of the room.

There was nothing to do but watch as the heavy oak door slammed shut and was bolted on the far side.

Logan let out a long breath, staring across the room at Ashley. She was absolutely composed—the only hint of fear had been in the slight strain of her voice, as if it was a battle to keep it steady. That, and the flash of panic in her eyes when the man had thrown a knife at his head. The rest of it—the simpering female—had been an obvious act.

She held his gaze for a moment and then nodded. "Okay. Let's get out of here."

"How are we going to do that, exactly?" He looked up at the rope knotted around his hands, looped over the hook. Too high for him to stretch and pull himself free. The tied ankles didn't help, either. And Ashley... well, she wasn't getting out of that chair anytime soon.

A small scraping noise pulled his attention back to her. Using her feet, she was part jumping, part sliding the chair toward him.

"If I can get close enough, maybe you can use the chair to unhook your hands."

"And," he recollected, "I've got a knife in my shirt pocket."

She slid the chair another foot closer, so painfully slowly. "I thought we weren't allowed to bring weapons across the border."

"It's got a two-inch blade." He rolled his eyes. "It hardly counts as a weapon. Besides, you never know when a Swiss army knife will come in handy."

Finally, Ashley managed to slide the chair right up to his knees. Using his aching abdominal muscles, he hoisted his tied feet up onto the edge of the chair and pushed off, simultaneously lifting the rope around his wrists off the hook. His sudden weight on the chair sent both it and Ashley rocking precariously, but she didn't tip.

"That feels so much better." He rotated his shoulders to get the blood circulating again and gingerly touched his side. A couple of bruised ribs, but nothing felt broken.

"Good. Then get me out of this chair." Her dark eyes sparked. She had more guts than half the park rangers he'd worked with, and this was her first job in the field. Something inside his chest swelled.

"You're a real magnet for trouble, you know that?" He fished the knife out of his pocket and worked the blade open. "And the worst part is, you seem to like it."

"Like it?" she scoffed. "I won't like it if they come back here while you're dawdling around with that knife."

"Maybe I should leave you tied up, if you're going to complain."

She gave him a crooked smile, watching as Logan carefully maneuvered the sharp blade against the ropes binding his wrists. In a matter of minutes he had sawed through the coil and unraveled the bonds. After freeing his ankles, he worked on the ropes securing Ashley's feet and upper body to the chair.

She stood, holding out her hands so he could free her wrists. "You're pretty proficient at this. Do you get captured often?"

"No, never done it before." He gave her a wry grin. "I have you to thank for this pleasure."

He took both her hands—so soft and warm—in one of his, holding as he sawed at the rope with the knife. As the last of the binding came loose, Logan pulled it from her wrists to reveal bright red chafing marks on her skin. Anger surged in his gut and he looked up at her, searching her face.

"They didn't touch you, did they?" He'd been pretty delirious after that knock to the head. No telling what might've happened while he was out.

"No." Her cheeks flushed. "But what about you? How's your head?"

He shrugged. "It hurts."

His heart skipped as she brushed her fingertips lightly against the back of his head, gently moving his hair. Something shifted in her brown eyes, her brows raising in the center.

"You've got a big knot." Her throat bobbed. "We'd better watch for signs of concussion." She smiled wryly. "I know all about them."

"Yes, you do." Logan cleared his throat, torn between the need to comfort her and to punch the men who had hurt her. But neither would help at the moment—they still needed to escape. "First, let's get out of here."

"I noticed the roof looked pretty dilapidated from the outside—do you think we could find a place to climb out?"

"Maybe." He paced the room, assessing the ceiling.

"The adobe is probably at least a foot thick. It would take a long time to carve our way out unless we find a weak spot."

She pointed to a section along the back wall where bits of adobe had broken loose. "What about there? Along the beam?"

Logan grabbed the chair and walked over to the spot. Climbing up, he scraped along the crevice with his knife. "The beam is called a *viga*, incidentally, and these—" he pointed to smaller crossbeams "—are called *latillas*."

Ashley tapped her foot impatiently. "I guess I know who to ask the next time I want a lesson on adobe construction. Now, can we get out through there or not?"

Logan shot her a quick scowl as he dug his knife into the adobe above his head. "This might work. If you can muster a little more patience, I'll try to cut us a hole. Keep an eye on that door."

Digging through the hardened mud was slow work, but a steady trickle of dust and small pieces kept falling to the floor. A large chunk of mud and straw broke free, crashing to the ground near the base of the chair.

"I think I'm through." He wiped dust away from his face using his forearm. A patch of blue sky peeked through the newly opened hole.

"What's going on in there?" Someone drew back the door latch with a heavy thud.

"Ashley," Logan whispered, "over here. I can get you out."

"Too late." She shook her head, pressing herself against the wall beside the door.

The door that was opening as José walked in, holding a gun.

TWELVE

Ashley knew she'd have a split-second advantage as José's eyes adjusted to the dark room. She waited, holding her breath, as he stepped inside, his gun arm outstretched.

She made her move as soon as he had taken a full step inside the doorway, seizing his arm and rotating the weapon backward and out of his hand. Before he could cry out, she jerked his arm around behind his back and dropped him to the floor. Pressing her knee into his back, she trained the gun on his head. "Don't move. And don't make a sound. Logan, bring me a rope."

Logan, who was staring at her openmouthed, jumped down off the chair and brought the rope, helping her to tie José's hands behind his back. "You didn't learn that in NPS training."

A statement, not a question. So much for working undercover. But now wasn't the time to talk about her real identity.

He cut off a strip of cloth from the hem of his shirt and wrapped it around José's mouth. "Better gag him, too, just to be safe."

"Your boss isn't going to be too happy," Ashley said to the bound man, cinching another rope around his ankles. She glanced up at Logan, nodding at the door. "Is it clear?"

He looked out but then slid the door shut. "Guards pacing the perimeter. And the American will be back any minute. We've got a better chance on the roof."

"All right." Ashley stood, tucking José's gun into her waistband. Forget the Mexican laws. Their lives were on the line.

She followed Logan over to the chair underneath the hole he had carved into the ceiling. He jumped up onto it and a minute later expanded the hole wide enough to allow her shoulders through.

"Ladies first." His expression allowed no room for argument. "You can help me from up there. Stay low to the roof and close to the back wall so they don't see you from below."

Ashley nodded.

"When he comes back empty-handed," Logan continued, "he's going to be after blood. I don't want you anywhere near here. If you see anyone coming, get yourself as far away from here as you can."

"I'm not leaving you behind, so stop talking and help me up. I'll wait for you on the roof."

"No, you'll run if I tell you to." Logan's gaze was unyielding. "I'm training you, remember? That makes me in charge." He reached down to help her onto the chair.

Ashley took his hand and climbed up, finding herself suddenly only inches away from him. Her knees buckled a bit and she reached out a quick hand for the back of the chair. In response, Logan wrapped a steadying arm around her waist.

Avoiding eye contact and doing her best to keep her heart rate from skyrocketing, she said a bit breathlessly, "Okay, I'm ready. Lift me up."

"Try to keep your weight on the beams. Who knows how weak the rest of the adobe is."

Placing both hands on her waist, Logan lifted until she could squeeze her arms and shoulders out through the hole. Using the *viga* to support her weight, she carefully maneuvered the rest of her body until she was fully out in the bright, hot, sunshine.

Crouching low to the roof, Ashley glanced over the presidio. She let out a quick breath. No movement. She peeked back into the hole. "The coast looks clear so far. Let's get you out."

They both started digging through the adobe, Logan with his knife, Ashley scratching with her nails until her fingertips were raw. Finally the hole looked big enough to squeeze his broad shoulders through.

"Now what?" she asked. "How do we get you out?"

"Lie down and give me your hands. I can pull myself up, but you've got to hold on tight until I reach the exposed wood."

She did as he instructed, already feeling the sweat building on her palms. No pressure. She could do this... How much did he weigh, anyway?

Logan squeezed her hands, looking up at her in his steadfast way. "You can do this. Ready?"

Fortifying herself with a deep breath, Ashley tightened her grip on his hands. "Ready."

With a sudden strain on her arms, Logan heaved himself upward, using the back of the chair as extra leverage to help him gain enough height to reach the exposed log. The force of his weight on the chair back caused it to tip, until his feet were dangling in the air. He released one of her hands to find a handhold on the beam. For a split second, she thought he might fall, but at the last moment he dug his fingers into the wood.

She helped direct his other hand to the wood and waited as he pulled his head out through the hole, a crooked grin on his dusty face.

"Thanks," he said, puffing with exertion. The tendons and muscles in his lower arms could have been carved out of rock.

"Anytime." She dipped her chin in a quick nod.

Soon his upper body was through the hole. He was swinging up his other leg when voices below made them freeze. Ashley tensed, casting him an anxious glance.

Logan held a finger to his lips and motioned to the upper wall of the presidio running parallel to the roof. She followed him over to the wall and they ran along it toward the west end of the complex.

They had only gone a short distance when they heard the oak door open below. Almost immediately, shouting broke out, followed by random gunshots into the adobe roof.

Throwing caution to the wind, they stumbled ahead as fast as they could for the far wall of the complex. A voice called out from the courtyard below. Ashley ducked lower as bullets whizzed past her head.

A second later the shooting stopped. Two men climbed up onto the roof in pursuit. She didn't recognize one of them, but the other was the American she'd sent on the fool's errand to find the map. She could see the rage etched on his face from all the way across the roof.

She and Logan reached the far wall as the pursuing men opened fire. Logan cupped his hands for her to step up and she pulled herself onto the wall. Large chunks of adobe broke loose and fell on the far side as she scrambled to maintain her balance.

Logan hoisted himself up next to her, narrowly avoiding a gunshot to the leg, and grabbed her hand. "We have to jump."

A wave of horror crashed through her insides as she surveyed the huge drop on the far side. Fifteen, twenty feet? Enough to make her head swim.

But Logan yanked on her arm, shouting, "Now!"

In an instant she catapulted into the air, her stomach finding its way up into her throat, her legs scrambling to brace for impact.

A second later they hit the sand. Ashley's legs absorbed the brunt of the blow, but momentum carried her forward until she fell facedown into the scorching sand.

Logan was already pulling on her again, urging her to run.

The men hadn't jumped, but bullets bit into the sand at her feet. Pulling José's gun from her waistband, she fired a couple of shots in their direction before sprinting toward the river and the hope of safety.

Logan raced for the river, still in a partial state of shock at the way Ashley had taken down José like it was a training exercise. Even now, as they tore across the rough terrain, her face was a mask of concentration.

He zigzagged around the scrubby desert brush, his feet sinking deep into the sand with each step. Exertion stole the oxygen from his lungs, making his legs burn. And it was even harder for Ashley, who wasn't used to the heat or the landscape.

Yet there she was, barely lagging, in better physical condition than most park rangers.

Something about her wasn't adding up.

Gunfire sounded behind them again, another reminder now was not the time to ask.

"Where…are…we…going?" Ashley's question came out between gasps for air.

Logan had already been considering the answer as they ran toward the Rio Grande. The shouting and gunshots receded and he slowed the pace as they forced their way through the thick grasses and reeds near the river's edge.

"After we cross the river," he panted, "we'll try to lose them in the trees as we make our way back to the park's main road."

She nodded. "What about water?"

"The rangers keep a cache nearby, maybe a mile away. But we don't really have a choice."

"No, we don't." She gnawed her lip. "But I'd rather risk doubling back to San Vicente than turning into dinner for the turkey vultures. The river road isn't even paved, is it?"

Logan shook his head. "No. But we do patrol it. Prayerfully we'll meet a ranger before we have to walk all the way to Rio Grande Village."

The absence of gunfire suggested they hadn't been seen yet, but it was only a matter of time before their pursuers found their tracks. Taking Ashley's hand, Logan crept into the center of the river where the water was waist deep and the current was stronger. A bullet zinged past his shoulder.

Seconds later three men scrambled down the slope toward the river, shooting wildly as they came.

"Duck!" Logan called.

Ashley dived under in the nick of time, a bullet skipping past where she had been a heartbeat before.

The three men reached the river's edge. Two of them charged into the water while the other raised his weapon and fired.

Logan lunged forward. Searing pain ripped across his upper left arm as he kicked into a dive under the murky water. Bracing the injured arm against his side, he used the other arm to swim with the current, staying under as long as possible.

Surfacing with a splutter, he scanned the surface for Ashley. Her head bobbed downstream twenty yards ahead. They had traveled far enough that their entry point, with the solitary shooter, was now out of sight.

But the other two were still in the water somewhere behind them, firing as soon as Logan surfaced. He dove under again, accelerating to catch Ashley. His arm ached so badly it was impossible to use. But she was kicking against the current to wait for him and a moment later the current swept him to her position.

"There are two of them in the river behind us," he said, swimming alongside her.

"There." Ashley pointed downstream to a cluster of bushes on the US bank.

"Perfect."

They both kicked hard, trying to gain distance on their pursuers before reaching the bushes. Ashley fired off shots upstream to distract their pursuers as she and Logan clambered onto the grainy, wet sand.

Logan flung himself underneath one of the prickly bushes, pulling Ashley down beside him. She held the gun out, at the ready, as they waited.

The leafy undergrowth obscured much of their view of the river, but they watched in silence as two heads bobbed past, facing downstream.

Logan let out a long breath. "Praise God." He rolled onto his back. His arm throbbed mercilessly, and he hated to think about how many bacteria had just washed into the wound. But at least they were alive.

"You can say that again." Ashley propped herself up onto her elbows. "Now what?"

She glanced over her shoulders, as if assessing their options. But when her gaze swept across Logan, she stopped, her dark eyes filling with alarm.

"Logan, what is it? You're white as a sheet." She stared down at the sand between them, stained red from his blood. "You've been hit."

"My shoulder." He pointed across his body. "I'll be fine. Right now, we need to get away from the river before they decide to double back." Every word was becoming harder to get out as the pain radiated from his shoulder down through his upper chest and side. He hadn't even looked at it yet, but part of him felt nauseous just thinking about it. He had never done well with personal injuries.

It was much better to think about getting away.

Ashley watched him a moment longer, her brow compressed with concern. She checked over her shoulder again. "Still clear."

She crawled out from under the bush and crouched behind it, waiting as Logan gingerly slid out.

Her eyes went wide. "Your shirtsleeve is soaked with blood."

"Don't tell me that right now." Logan gritted his teeth against a wave of nausea. He nodded toward the north. "By my reckoning, we traveled half a mile down the river. That gives us about another quarter mile until we reach a couple of backcountry sites and the water cache. Keep low and behind the bushes as much as possible."

Ashley nodded. "All right, but we're going to look at that arm as soon as we get to the water. Got it?"

"Yes, ma'am."

And then maybe he'd finally get some answers as to how she'd taken out an armed man like it was her job.

THIRTEEN

Logan set out in the direction of the water cache, crouching low and dodging from bush to bush. It'd only be a matter of time before their pursuers decided to double back. Ashley stayed right behind him, gun at the ready.

As they approached the first campsite, he scoured the tree line for the telltale color of a tent. Nothing.

Ashley stopped beside him inside the cover of the trees. "See anyone?"

He shook his head, pointing. "The water cache is up that dirt road, toward River Road East."

Cautiously he led the way along the edge of the brush toward the large metal box serving as the cache.

Ashley tugged at the lock that secured the door.

"I've got the key." He fished into his pocket, breathing a quick prayer of thanks that his key ring had survived their river excursion.

He opened the door, revealing several gallons of water. He pulled two jugs out, setting them on the ground as Ashley rummaged through the first-aid kit. After relocking the box, they found a nearby copse of cottonwood trees that would offer some degree of protection.

Finding a patch of grass shielded by overhanging

brush, he collapsed onto the ground. Ashley sat nearby, opening one of the gallons and offering it to him.

He waved her off. "You first."

She took a long drink before handing it back. "Mmm, 150-degree water. Too bad I didn't think to bring a tea bag." She wiped her lips with the back of her hand.

Logan chuckled. "Hey, out in here in the desert, this is liquid gold. Don't complain."

"We probably already swallowed enough river water to die of dysentery." She frowned.

"You survived just fine the last time you went swimming in the Rio Grande." Setting down the water, he gingerly touched the aching place on his left arm with his free hand, fresh blood coming away on his fingertips.

Ashley pulled his hand back. "Let me help you." The words were gentle and soft, like her touch.

He watched her as she examined the wound. The way her wet hair fell against the curve of her cheek. Long lashes framing thoughtful eyes. The sweet, subtle scent of berries that made it hard to concentrate when she was near.

Had he ever seen anyone so beautiful? And it wasn't only physical beauty. There was something about her— her inner strength and courage, the intelligence and compassion behind those eyes—that grabbed him deep inside. Made him want to protect her, even though she clearly didn't need his help.

Before he could stop himself, he reached out to brush a finger against her cheek. He expected her to shy away, but instead her gaze turned to his. The depths of her eyes mirrored the same turmoil of emotions tucked inside his chest. Awareness. Fear. Longing. Hope. Was there love? Could there be so quickly?

His throat closed, seized with panic, and he jerked his

hand back, inadvertently sending another shudder of pain through his body at the rapid movement.

Erin. For one brief, glorious moment he'd forgotten entirely about her and the way she'd shattered his heart.

He forced a deep breath. No matter what feelings were flitting through his chest, he couldn't act on them. Ashley had her own secrets and one day she would leave the same way Erin had. Hadn't he learned his lesson the first time?

Pushing the unsettling thoughts aside, he glanced at Ashley. She'd turned her attention back to his arm, but a flicker of hurt crossed her features before she pressed her lips together into a thin line. Irritated at him? Somehow, Logan didn't think so.

A relationship wasn't something either of them could afford right now, especially when it was guaranteed to fail.

He'd have to try harder, much harder, if he was going to protect them both.

When Ashley spoke again, her tone was even. "It looks like the bullet only grazed you, but the wound is deep. Your deltoid is torn and you're still losing blood."

"Deltoid? What are you, an undercover medical doctor?" he asked, half laughing, half grimacing.

Ashley didn't laugh. "Not exactly."

"What then?"

She didn't meet his gaze. "I'm going to rip off part of your sleeve, so I can clean this."

Avoiding the question? One way or another, he was going to get the truth out of her.

When she poured water over the wound, washing away sand and debris from the river, he bit his tongue in pain. "That…really…hurts…" he said through gritted teeth.

"I know." She smiled faintly, her eyes full of compassion. "And we haven't even gotten to the isopropanol yet." She held up a small bottle from the first-aid kit.

Logan groaned.

"Here. Squeeze my hand."

It fit perfectly inside his larger one, as if she belonged there with him. He kept his focus on their hands, even as his shoulder caught fire and red flamed in front of his vision.

A moment later she pulled her hand away. "All done. I've gotten as much dirt out as I can."

"You mean I won't die of a strep infection?"

"You're going to be fine." It took a couple of minutes more for her to bind the wound with a roll of sterile gauze. Using the rest of his shirt as a sling, she secured the injured arm to his side.

"Thank you. I'm glad you paid attention during first aid."

She gave him a crooked smile. "I bet you didn't think your training job would be so easy."

"You call this easy?" He held up his hand and she pulled him to his feet.

He felt better after the rest, but not as strong as he would've liked, especially since they might have to walk several more miles if a car didn't drive by.

Ashley stayed beside him, ready to help if he needed it. Her shoulders were tense, her face wary, as she watched the surrounding foliage for any sign of their pursuers.

After they had reached the unpaved road along the river, Logan broke the silence. "Can I ask you something?"

"Of course." Her dark brows pulled together, head tilting to one side.

"Who are you?"

* * *

Ashley swallowed, staring at her feet as she trudged up the dusty road. "I'm sorry I put you in danger." She glanced at him after a long moment.

"That wasn't what I asked." His face was pale and drawn from the injury, but his eyes were drilling a hole through her head.

No choice but to trust him now. If he was working for Jimenez, if he was the inside man, he'd just blown several perfect opportunities to kill her. And unless she left the park, she was going to keep placing his life in danger.

He deserved to know why.

"My real name is Ashley Thompson. I'm an agent for the Federal Bureau of Investigation." She glanced sharply at him, waiting for some kind of response, but he merely watched her, his gaze unreadable. "I was sent here undercover to track Rico Jimenez."

He was quiet for a long moment. "I've heard of Jimenez. He's a cartel boss. But why are you *here*? I thought he operated mainly to the west, south of Arizona."

"Not anymore. At least, not according to FBI intel."

"And those men in San Vicente, you think they're part of his cartel?"

"Yes." She gnawed at her lip. Might as well come out with all of it. "The reason I wanted to go to San Vicente wasn't for the chapel. I had to meet a contact. Jimenez must've found out and sent those men after us."

His eyes narrowed. "When did you meet with this contact? I was with you the whole time." His gaze drifted to her arm, the one no longer carrying a souvenir blanket, and he raised his brows. "Ah. The shopping. Now that makes more sense."

She nodded. "I met him behind the chapel while you

were taking pictures." She filled him in briefly on what the man had said. "Jimenez is working the mine."

Logan shook his head. "No, not possible. No way he could keep something like that secret, even in a remote place like this."

She arched an eyebrow. "Oh, really? Dick Barclay gave me a file on him, and it was almost empty. But my file from the FBI contains *pages* of tips we've received of his activity through this park. He's doing it, all right, and he's doing it right under our noses."

He frowned. "But why are you here undercover? Why didn't the feds tell us?"

"I asked myself the same thing, until I pieced it together from the files on my laptop. He's got someone on the inside, Logan. How else could he be smuggling drugs and cartel members through here without being caught? That's why I couldn't say anything to you. Barclay and Ed Chambers think I'm here undercover to avoid scaring Jimenez off, but the real reason is to find the mole in the park service."

He ran his good hand through his hair, turning even paler. "That explains a few things." His green gaze was steady. "Thank you for trusting me."

"Well—" her lips tipped up "—if it was your job to get rid of me, you've failed miserably."

"The last thing I want to do is get rid of you." The gentle tone of his voice made her cheeks flush. "Does this mean you'll let me help you?"

"I've already put you in enough danger." Her chest constricted. "Besides, Barclay threatened to tell my boss about the head injury if I didn't bring him hard proof of Jimenez's activity. I've got nothing to report so far other than nearly getting both of us killed." She gestured at Logan's chest. "And losing a National Park Service camera."

"Jimenez's thugs stole it." He raised an eyebrow. "That hardly counts as losing it. Besides, we still have the map. We even know what trail to search, thanks to your contact. And we've seen the view from San Vicente. I'm sure I can dig up some photographs from the archives to help us narrow the search radius."

"You're just trying to make me feel better."

"Is it working?" The skin around his eyes crinkled as he grinned.

"Maybe." Ashley smiled back. "You're not mad at me?"

"For what?"

"Lying to you about who I am."

"No. You were doing your job. I probably would've done the same thing." He cocked his head to one side, eyeing her for a moment. "But what about the memory loss? The first day I met you? Did you remember any of this?"

She shook her head. "I figured it out when I got home to Panther Junction and found my badge. But I couldn't tell you. Even though I wanted to…" Her voice trailed away, remembering both the frustrating darkness in her mind and how much she'd wanted to trust Logan. A part of her felt very glad he knew the truth now.

His hand slipped around hers, rough and warm and comfortable, and a tangle of emotions fluttered through her chest.

"Thank you for telling me now. I want to help you." He gave her hand a squeeze and then released it, leaving her fingers cold despite the afternoon heat.

"I know." But how could he help? Realistically, Barclay would be on the phone with Morton the second he heard about what had happened today.

Logan cut into her thoughts. "Do you remember anything more about what happened to you that first day?"

"No. And I can't think of any reason why I would even be driving down there." So frustrating, these remaining bits of missing information. She frowned. "I've got this nagging feeling it has something to do with my brother. But that doesn't make any sense."

They walked in silence for a few moments. She kept glancing at Logan, at the way his brows knit together in concentration. Processing everything she'd told him.

He kicked a rock. Stared at his boots. Ran a hand through his hair. Stared at the horizon. When he finally looked at her again, he wouldn't hold her gaze. "I might have an idea." He hesitated. "You said your brother's name was Sam, right? Sam Thompson?"

"Yes." Why was Logan looking at her like that?

"Do you remember what he did? Where he worked?"

She thought for a long moment. "It's not DC. Somewhere else, far away. At first, I could only remember him being in school, but that would've been two years ago." She frowned. "Why are you asking?" And why was he using past tense?

Logan kept watching her, waiting, as if he knew the answer already and wanted her to work it out for herself.

"What?" she asked impatiently.

He pressed his lips together. "I think I knew him, Ashley. If it's the same Sam Thompson, I think he worked here."

She stared at Logan, not sure she'd heard him correctly. "But...how? How could you know him?" Something twisted inside her chest—the same feeling she had every time she looked at his photograph. Or remembered that she wasn't on speaking terms with God.

"It might not be the same man," Logan said quietly.

"But we lost a ranger about three months ago. His name was Sam Thompson. He was young—early twenties. One of the most joyful people I've ever met."

"'Lost him'?" She repeated the words slowly, her brain struggling to catch up. Dead? She shook her head. "Sam's still alive. He couldn't be the same person. I know…"

Her voice dwindled away as images flung themselves into her conscious mind. A phone call and a broken drinking glass, crystal splinters scattered across the tile of her apartment floor… Her mother clutching her father and weeping like her heart had split in two… A closed wooden casket and a church full of people dressed in black…

She pressed her hand to her mouth, stifling the sob trying to choke her. Her throat burned, tears stinging her eyes.

"I'm sorry." Logan wrapped his good arm around her back, pulling her to his chest. "I'm so sorry. Those aren't the good memories to get back."

"I don't…" She swallowed but the lump wouldn't go away. Burying her face into Logan's shirt didn't help. "I don't know what happened. How could I forget?"

He stroked her hair, his touch gentle and soothing. "It was only three months ago, Ashley. Your brain is still healing."

"What…what happened to him?" So hard to breathe. As if someone had dropped a heavy rock on her chest.

"He didn't come back from patrol. We sent out a search-and-rescue team, and…" His voice trailed away, his eyes full of raw emotion. Whatever had happened, he hadn't recovered from it yet.

"And?" she prompted softly.

"We…" He swallowed. "I…found the body a half mile off the trail. He didn't have any water with him. He'd wandered off the trail, gotten lost without proper supplies…and…we were too late." Logan's voice cracked.

Ashley dug her forehead back into his shirt, shaking her head. It shouldn't be true and yet… His words struck a chord of truth deep inside her. Hadn't she felt sick to her stomach every time she looked at pictures of Sam?

Latent memories of him trickled into her mind. His laughter. All the lame jokes he used to tell. His insistence on going to church every week. His love of camping and the outdoors… Suddenly she could picture him in a ranger's uniform. Maybe he *had* worked here. But—

"No," she insisted. "That couldn't have been Sam. It must have been someone else. He was an expert outdoorsman. He never would've gone out unprepared."

"Maybe it wasn't your brother. I don't know. But I do know the desert is a harsh place and even experts have underestimated it before."

"But wasn't he trained? I mean, you all wouldn't have sent him out alone if he didn't know the trails or know how much water to carry, right?"

Logan didn't meet her eyes as he answered. "No, we wouldn't have. A rookie ranger can't go on patrol alone until their trainer verifies they're ready."

"So…what, then?" Ashley asked sharply. Anger felt so much better than the misery of grief. "Someone sent him out too soon? Who trained him?"

Logan stared straight ahead down the road, a muscle twitching in his jaw.

After a long time he turned to her and Ashley's breath caught at the storm of sorrow and self-reproach in his eyes.

"I did."

FOURTEEN

"Oh, Logan." All the anger had melted out of her voice. She pulled away from his chest and laid a hand on his arm. Logan had to resist the overwhelming urge to pull away from the touch meant to comfort. He didn't deserve comfort. "It couldn't have been your fault. You're excellent at what you do."

"Would you still say that if you knew for sure it was your brother?"

She looked down at the dirt. "I have his picture at home, in Panther Junction. I'll show it to you when we get back."

If *we get back*, Logan thought. Sometimes no amount of knowing about a place was enough to guarantee survival. He and Ashley might end up meeting the same fate as Sam—dehydration and heat stroke.

He hadn't said anything to Ashley, but he was feeling worse the longer they walked. There might come a point where he would have to send her on alone, without his help—a terrifying thought. Whether the Big Bend Sam had been her brother or not, Logan didn't think he could take losing another ranger that way.

And the closer the sun got to the horizon, the more their chances of spending the night out here increased.

When he stumbled over a rock in the path, Ashley glanced up at him, a crease forming between her brows. "How much farther is it to the main road?"

"Longer than I'd like," he admitted. "Maybe two or three miles. But the hot spring site is closer, maybe a mile from here."

"Will anyone be there this time of day?"

He sighed. "Hit or miss. It's popular with tourists, but it's also right on the river. We might run into the shooters."

"I think it's a chance we'll have to take." She took his good arm in hers. "Let me help you."

They didn't talk much over the next half hour. Logan concentrated on each step, one foot in front of the other, and the steady support of the woman beside him.

The sun had become a giant orange ball dipping behind the Chisos Mountains by the time Logan caught sight of the low buildings that marked the hot spring. The natural spring of hot water, located right next to the Rio Grande, had been discovered and used by early European settlers hundreds of years ago. A small town had sprung up at one point, complete with a general store and post office. But, like most small towns in so remote an area, its lifetime had been short-lived and now only a few ramshackle, abandoned buildings remained.

The park service had built a parking lot near the old town and a trail to the hot spring itself, a few hundred yards away near the river. It was a favorite swimming hole for park visitors, but not usually this late in the day.

He hadn't expected anyone to be there, but that didn't prevent the disappointment that washed over him anyway as they walked past the hot spring and up to the trail leading to the parking lot.

"It'll be another two miles from here to the main road." He struggled to keep his voice even.

"We can do it." Ashley smiled encouragingly, but the creases lingered between her eyes.

They rounded the bend leading past the old post office. Suddenly slamming car doors broke the silence. Two engines started, one after the other. One of the vehicles pulled away immediately, but the other idled for one precious moment.

Ashley's gaze darted to his.

Logan pulled his arm away. "Run."

She raced up the slope toward the paved lot, waving her arms and yelling so loudly they'd certainly be shot if their pursuers were anywhere nearby.

But then he crested the hill behind her and saw a truck. And—*oh, thank You, Lord*—it was the dark green of the park service. But it was almost out of the parking lot.

"Stop!" Ashley yelled, waving her arms and chasing it from behind.

The truck slammed into Reverse and pulled to a stop a short distance away. The door opened.

Ed Chambers. Logan's legs went weak as relief flooded his insides. He sank to his knees and waited as Ashley and the chief ranger ran over to him.

"Ed…"

"Hey, brother." Ed knelt. "Looks like you got yourself into a bit of a tussle. I can't wait to hear the story."

Logan arched his eyebrows. "It's pretty exciting…"

"I'm sure it is. You can tell me about it on the way to the clinic. Ashley, help me get him to the truck."

Ashley slid into the center of the truck's single bench seat and helped Logan into the passenger seat. Ed climbed in behind the wheel.

The distance to Terlingua was excruciatingly long: an hour up past Panther Junction, plus another out to the west entrance.

As they drew near to Panther Junction, Ed glanced at Ashley. "I imagine you'll want to come to Terlingua, too. Otherwise, I can drop you off here."

Logan could swear red tinted Ashley's cheeks. Ed did have a knack for reading the human heart.

Graciously, Ed continued, "You might need to get looked at, too. Seems like you've had quite a day out there."

His friend had *no* idea.

Ashley and Ed had been sitting in the waiting room at the Terlingua medical center for a good hour. A nurse had examined Ashley and, after painfully removing at least a dozen cactus spines and cleaning out several cuts, she'd offered some ibuprofen and released her. Now, as they waited for Logan, Ashley shared as many details as she could. Ed already knew she was with the FBI and searching for Jimenez, but she didn't tell him about the map or her real motive for being undercover.

"So, what did they want from you?" Ed scratched his forehead.

Ashley shrugged. She hated lying to him, almost as much as she had hated lying to Logan. But she still didn't know whom she could trust, and she certainly didn't want to put anyone else in danger. "Somehow they knew we were with the park service. I think they wanted to find out how much we knew. If we were on to them or not."

Ed nodded. "This is bad news for us, for the park. If word leaks out that a cartel is operating through here, we'll lose our tourists, even after Jimenez is long gone."

"We don't have any proof yet," Ashley cautioned. The

last thing she wanted was to scare Jimenez off before she and Logan found the mine. She hoped today's escape wouldn't be enough to do so.

"But you have the tips that brought you here in the first place. And your contact. Did he give you any details on where Jimenez is operating?"

Nothing she could share. Especially before she figured out who the insider was in the park service. "Nothing we can act on quite yet. I need to discuss this with my supervisor at the Bureau before we do anything."

"All right," Ed agreed. "But if we find those gunmen on this side of the Rio Grande, I'm arresting them."

"Fair enough."

"How much does Logan know about you?"

Ashley got the feeling the question pertained as much to his friend's well-being as it did to the safety of her mission. "Everything." Finally, something she didn't have to lie about. "I couldn't keep it a secret anymore."

He stared at the empty plastic chairs across the room for a moment, his expression thoughtful. But then his features relaxed into a grin. "Well, you chose wisely. I'd trust that man with my life."

"I know." She studied her hands. If only things could be different. If only she and Logan could have met under normal circumstances, not in this web of intrigue and danger.

"He's had his heart broken before." Ed's soft words pulled her out of her reverie. "He's a good man, but you have to be patient with him."

"Why are you telling me this?" She cocked her head to the side.

"Because I can see something's there, between the two of you. It's taken him a long time to get over the past."

"I…" She started to deny it but gave up. If it was so

obvious Ed could see it, there wasn't any point in lying to him. Or to herself, for that matter.

Ed smiled. "He'd probably kill me if he knew I told you that."

"Told her what?" Logan stood at the entrance to the waiting room. His arm was bandaged and secured in a proper sling, and his face had some of its regular color back. A smile played on his lips, at odds with his narrowed eyes.

"That you are the most stubborn, toughest ranger I've ever had the pleasure of working with." Ed rose to his feet and clapped Logan on his good arm.

"They say I'll live. And they didn't even have to amputate." Logan shot them a lopsided grin. "Thanks to you two."

"I'm just grateful Ed was at the hot spring," Ashley said.

"God was very merciful to us." Logan shook his head.

As much as Ashley wanted to leave God out of the equation, she had to agree the timing had been downright providential. Another minute later and they would've missed Ed entirely.

"What were you doing there, anyway, Ed?" Logan asked as they headed for the exit.

He shrugged. "I had a meeting with Adam Smith to talk about opening up the old post office and general store for visitors." Glancing at Ashley, he added, "He's the chief of resource management."

Ed turned back to Logan. "I was there all afternoon. Your girl here caught me seconds before I drove off. I'm glad you weren't any later."

Ashley frowned as she thought about what could have happened. Catching Ed's reference to her, she glanced up to see Logan's eyes go wide. For one moment she imagined what it would be like to be with someone like him—respected, loved, secure. An equal, valued partner. She'd put her career first for so long, she'd never realized what she was missing.

Her heart hurt. Maybe someday.

Right now, she had a case to solve.

She cleared her throat. "It's late. We'd better get back to headquarters."

The heat of the day had faded into a cool desert night by the time they arrived at Panther Junction.

"I'll talk to the superintendent about what happened," Ed said. "You two get some rest. I don't want to see either of your faces skulking around the park tomorrow, got it? Logan, you need to give that arm a chance to heal, so I want you to take off a couple of days, at least. I'm sure the superintendent will agree with me."

"Maybe a day or two," Logan said begrudgingly. "But I don't want to be left out of the loop."

"Don't worry, I'll keep you informed." Ed waved good-night.

"He's right, you know." The first stars glittered above as Ashley and Logan strolled toward his house. "You do need time to recover." She tapped her temple. "Especially with the head injury."

"I can't let you go looking for that mine alone and, if I know you, that's exactly what you'll do while I'm lying around on my couch resting."

"I guess you know me pretty well." She grinned. "But if it makes you feel any better, I don't know where to look yet. All I've got is the trail name."

"How about if we try to track down some pictures in the archives? I'm not so incapacitated I can't at least do that."

She nodded. "All right. But sleep in tomorrow. I won't do anything stupid."

"Promise?"

"Pinky swear."

Logan held out his good hand and she hooked her little finger with his, sending a jolt of warmth up her arm. "I'm going to hold you to that."

They reached his house but Logan didn't turn toward his door. "I'm taking you home."

"You don't need to," Ashley protested, facing him. His sandy-brown hair stuck out at odd angles after the chaos of their day, and she was filled with the sudden urge to touch it. *Absolutely not.*

"I know. I want to." His eyes were gentle. Caring. But then he stared down at the sidewalk. "And I want to see your brother's picture."

Of course. *Of course.* She was letting her personal feelings get in the way of work again. Logan wanted to help her catch Jimenez and get her memories back. He had never communicated an interest in anything more—not with words, anyway—and even if he did... She wasn't interested. She couldn't be interested. The job came first.

Her front door was still locked. She exhaled slowly as she dug her key out of her pocket. Apparently whoever had tried to break in the first time hadn't gained the courage to try again. Either that or they were extremely good at replacing everything the way she had left it.

"Where is the map, anyway?" Logan sat on her sofa.

"I've been carrying it with me." She glanced down at her waist.

"I'm glad they didn't search you."

"Me, too." She stepped inside her bedroom, pulling the cloth pouch out of the place where it had rubbed against her skin all day, and brought the map and the picture of Sam back to the living room. "At least I put it in a plastic bag, so it wouldn't get wet. Learned my lesson after the Jeep incident."

She handed the picture to Logan. "I found it in my wallet. It took me too long to remember who he was."

"It's not because you didn't love him," he said softly, taking the picture from her. She could scarcely breathe as she waited for him to say something.

He stared at the snapshot for a long moment before looking up, his eyes glistening in the lamplight. "I'm so, so sorry, Ashley." His voice broke. "Sam told me he had a sister who lived in DC, but I never made the connection until I heard your real last name. He never gave us any details about you."

She bit her lip, letting out a painful laugh. "He knew better than to divulge any of my secrets." Probably the only reason she managed to convince Morton to let her come here undercover. Nobody knew they were related.

"We had a memorial service here, so none of us traveled to the funeral."

Her eyes burned, and Ashley impatiently wiped the tears away as she took the picture back. "He wasn't very old, was he? Younger than me."

"Twenty-three." Logan pressed his lips together.

"Just out of college, then." She tried to keep the bitterness out of her voice, but there was so much of it filling her heart. It wasn't fair.

"It should never have happened." He dragged his hand over his face, through his hair. "I never should have sent him out there alone."

She dropped onto the cushion beside him. "It wasn't your fault. I know you well enough to know you wouldn't have let Sam go unless you thought he was ready. And, like I said, Sam knew his way around the outdoors." She wiped again at her cheeks. "Whatever happened wasn't your fault."

"Thank you for saying that. I still feel like I failed him. Like I should have gotten there or found him sooner. There must've been something I could've done differently."

"You're not all-powerful, Logan. You can't hold yourself to that standard." She looked down at her lap. "But Someone else is and He *could* have saved my brother. He just…didn't care." She pursed her lips, clenching her teeth before any more of the ugliness inside spilled out. Logan didn't deserve it.

"Oh, Ashley." The agony in his eyes threatened to break her angry heart into a thousand shards. "Is that what you think? That God took him away because He doesn't care?"

The bubble of unshed tears formed a solid lump in Ashley's throat. She swallowed. "What I think doesn't matter. It doesn't change the facts. Sam is gone and it doesn't make any sense."

"No, it doesn't make any sense to *us*." His warm hand rested on her knee. "Grief is a terrible, unavoidable part of this life. But it doesn't change the fact that God loves us, so much He was willing to die for us. We may never know or understand why Sam died. But God wants us to trust Him. And to let Him comfort us."

She wiped at her cheeks again. Stupid tears. If she didn't get Logan out of there soon, she'd turn into an unhinged, blubbering mess. "I'm sorry. It's obviously been a long day. I need some rest."

He pulled his hand back. "Of course. Get some sleep. I'll find you in the morning. And, Ashley? Be safe, okay?

If anyone tries to get in here, you call me right away. Got it?"

She nodded. "I'll see you later, Logan."

The door latched shut with a soft click.

Gone. Sam was gone and there was nothing she could do about it. And though Logan's unwavering faith tugged at her heart, she could never trust God again, not the way Logan wanted her to.

Yet another reason she could never think of him as more than a colleague.

Ashley managed to flip the dead bolt into place and sink onto the couch before the tears she'd been holding back all night escaped.

FIFTEEN

No one tried to break in during the night, though Ashley had half expected it. She slept with the map inside her shirt and her gun under her pillow. It wasn't until almost morning that she finally fell into a deep sleep. Her first thoughts when she woke were of Sam.

Missing memories had come back in the night, spurred on by what she'd learned. She could picture Sam's excitement when he'd gotten the job out here. How she had promised to visit him, but several months had passed and she'd never done it.

Later, Sam. I'll be able to get away later. There had never been a good time.

Until now, when it was too late. Her mouth filled with the taste of bitterness again. Dwelling on the past wouldn't help.

At least she knew now why she'd fought to get this assignment. To be a little closer to her brother and to see the place he'd loved. The same way Logan loved it.

The new day was beautiful in its own way. Dewdrops on the cactus spines and thick succulents glittered like diamonds in the early morning sunlight. Ashley sucked in a lungful of the fresh, pure mountain air as she took the familiar path to headquarters.

Hopefully, Logan was still asleep. In the meantime, she needed to update Morton and find a way to stall Barclay. Three days had come and gone.

Sandy, the receptionist, smiled pleasantly as Ashley entered the air-conditioned building. "Dr. Barclay would like to see you in his office."

No surprise there. "Thanks." She forced a smile, trying to ignore the knot in her stomach.

She knocked on his door, which was already ajar, and peeked her head inside. "Dr. Barclay?"

Barclay sat behind his metal desk, eyes closed, fingers rubbing the bridge of his nose beneath his eyeglasses. He waved her inside without looking up.

She closed the door and stood, waiting, gnawing the inside of her cheek.

"Have a seat, Thompson." He watched her expectantly, waiting until she sat. Dark circles under his eyes testified to a bad night's sleep. "What happened yesterday?"

"I had to meet a contact," she began, telling him nearly verbatim the same story she'd given Ed, leaving out any details that could possibly trickle back to Jimenez and scare him off.

"Do you realize what a mess you've created? Shots fired at the border? Not to mention the property damage to one of their historical sites. How am I going to explain this to the Mexican government?"

Anger flared in her gut. "Dr. Barclay, those were Jimenez's men. Somehow they knew I'd be down there. What else were we supposed to do?"

"Avoid the situation in the first place, Agent Thompson." His eyes grew hard. "I told you to do your job and get out. Now you've created an international incident I'll have to smooth over with the local authorities."

"You gave me three days to give you proof," she insisted. "Well, here it is."

Barclay shook his head and something about his expression made her heart plunge. "Not good enough." He picked up the handset of his phone, pressing one of the buttons. "Here she is, Agent Morton."

Lead filled Ashley's stomach, but she accepted the receiver and pasted on a smile. "Sir? I've almost got the proof on Jimenez we need. Another twenty-four hours will be enough."

"And the other part of your mission?" Morton asked gruffly.

The mole. If only she had more to tell him—not that she could in front of Barclay. "No leads. Yet. But I'm close."

"Barclay will have my head," he grumbled. "But all right, Thompson. Twenty-four hours. Tell him I'm pulling you. Today's Friday. If you don't get what you need, be back here by Monday morning and we'll find another angle. Got it?"

"Yes, sir." She sighed heavily for effect. "I'll be back by Monday." She passed the receiver to Barclay, slumping in her seat.

His smile was smug. "And good riddance. Now go pack your bags and make your travel arrangements."

She stood, pressing her lips together to keep from smiling. With a salute at the door, she turned away to search for Logan.

"How long have you been down here?" Ashley appeared in the doorway to the archive room, her pretty lips quirked despite the way her forehead crinkled.

Logan shrugged. "An hour, maybe?" He hadn't exactly paid attention to the time. Sleep had been impossible once his pain meds had worn off, and he couldn't afford to spend the day doped up on whatever that was they'd prescribed for him. It made a whole lot more sense to come down to the basement of headquarters, where they stored all the archival material, and to get to work searching for the photographs they wanted.

"You were supposed to come find me." She pulled out the metal chair on the opposite side of his table and plopped down. "You were *supposed* to sleep in."

"I couldn't. You were with Barclay. Besides—" he gestured to the stack of cardboard document boxes on the table "—there's plenty to do. Might as well get started instead of squandering the day sleeping."

She scowled again. "You're going to work yourself into an early grave."

"I won't be alone." He gave her a pointed look, grinning when she rolled her eyes.

"So, what've you got?" She leaned forward over the table and scanned the open file spread out in front of him.

"Nothing yet. I started with the oldest boxes that might have photographs. We had some records from the 1920s, but nothing from San Vicente. Now I'm up to the 1950s." He thumbed through the files remaining in the top box, its label "San Vicente and Boquillas" cracking with age. "Here, try this one."

They worked in companionable silence, sifting through yellowed newspaper articles, old documents and black-and-white photographs.

"Wait a minute." Logan let out a whoosh of air. Finally, they were getting somewhere.

Ashley brushed hair out of her face and leaned across the table. "What've you got?"

He sorted through the old photographs, one after another. "The presidio. The marketplace." He held one up, grinning. "The chapel. Looks pretty much the same today." His pulse quickened.

A series of pictures followed in which the photographer had turned in a circle, capturing a panorama... "Here." He held it up triumphantly.

The Chisos range, as seen from the chapel steps, stared back at him from the photograph. A tiny "April 1957" was handwritten on the bottom right corner.

"And it's even springtime," he proclaimed, exultant.

She wiggled her fingers. "Let me see."

He stood, walked around the edge of the table, set down the photograph and swiveled the desk light closer. Together he and Ashley hunched over the picture, their shoulders touching, as he held a magnifying glass above it. The top of Lost Mine Peak was visible, along with portions of the south face stretching down into the V-shaped wedge made by Juniper Canyon.

He grinned at her like a kid on Christmas break.

Her dark eyes gleamed. So beautiful.

And so close. The air crackled between them. How easy it would be to give in to these wild feelings surging in his chest, to bridge the distance and kiss her.

Something shifted in her eyes and she averted her gaze back to the photograph.

Logan swallowed. What was *wrong* with him? Colleagues. Erin. Foolish heart. He cleared his throat and reached for a blank piece of paper. "Let's narrow this down to where the light would hit first."

After overlaying the paper on the image, he traced the outline of the mountain and the surrounding terrain. A spur of Pummel Peak, to the east, would obscure everything but the top two thousand feet or so as the sun rose. He shaded in the remaining area, comparing it again with the photograph. "What trail did your contact say they were using?"

Ashley spread out a park map and studied it, nibbling at one of her fingertips. "He said the access was from Pine Canyon Trail, but they're driving the gold out through Juniper Canyon. To here."

"Mariscal Mountain. One of the least accessible areas of the park." Logan traced the route with his pencil. "Maybe even using the old mercury mine as a base, though that's open to any tourists brave enough to off-road out there." He tapped the pencil on the table. "Nobody's reported anything suspicious."

"Think we can find the mine?" Her eyebrows lifted, but her expression fell as she surveyed his arm wrapped in its sling. "You can't go out there."

"I absolutely can. Reconnaissance only."

Her face lit up. "Deal."

The sun was high overhead and blazing hot as Ashley hoisted her pack onto her back and started down Pine Canyon Trail after Logan. She'd insisted on carrying the camera and all the water for the hike—a full gallon, even though they'd only be out here a couple of hours.

Already her shirt clung to her back with sweat, making it hard not to think of Sam. How exhausted, how hot, how thirsty he must have been. He was probably delirious by the end. She hadn't had the stomach to ask Logan about the condition his body had been in—whether the vultures or coyotes had found it.

The trail wound upward as it left the open desert plateau and entered Pine Canyon. Inside the steep walls, pinyon pines, oaks and maples replaced the cactuses of the open desert, providing welcome relief from the sun.

Logan slowed the pace as they neared Lost Mine Peak.

Jimenez's men could be anywhere—he was bound to have guards along this path. Shooting a couple of rangers would get him noticed by the park service, but still... Ashley wouldn't put anything past him.

They followed the path around a bend. A rocky slope rose steeply on the right. To the left, a small ridge diverged from the level of the path, increasing in elevation as it ran westward. The canyon narrowed considerably ahead but appeared to open again where the ridge curved away to the south and the path disappeared into the trees.

She stopped Logan, pointing at the ridge. "What do you think?" she whispered. "Could we see well enough from up there?"

He nodded. "Should give us a good view of the south face. And provide some cover."

"Let me go first, okay?"

He frowned, but moved aside, following Ashley as she picked her way up the ridge. After another half hour, they reached a place near the end of the ridge where it widened enough to provide a decent lookout—maybe a hundred feet from where the path below disappeared into the woods.

She and Logan crouched behind the cover of some scrubby bushes as she took off the pack and pulled out the camera. They both crawled forward—awkward for Logan with his bound arm—until they could see over the edge of the ridge. She spent several minutes snapping pictures with the digital camera, from the top of the peak to the trail below.

"See anything?" he whispered.

She shook her head. "Nothing. Hopefully, the pictures will help." She was about to suggest heading back when voices echoed off the canyon walls.

Logan stiffened beside her.

Craning her neck for a better view, she watched as three men emerged from an invisible cleft in the rock partway up the mountain face, maybe twenty feet east of where the path ended. The sun glinted off an AK-47 assault rifle slung over one of the men's backs. She zoomed in with the camera, snapping a series of shots. The one with the gun kept glancing down at the path and along the trail.

Beside her, Logan propped up a pair of binoculars with one hand. "To think that thing's been there this whole time," he whispered, "and we never knew."

"Surely this will be enough proof for Morton."

Ashley kept taking pictures until two of the men turned back inside the opening. The third, the one with the gun, picked his way down the mountainside to the trail fifty feet below. He pulled the rifle off his back and propped it up against one shoulder as he started down the trail to the east, in the direction of the trailhead.

She exchanged a glance with Logan. "Now what?"

His forehead crinkled into a frown. "They can't be patrolling this trail like that all the time. Otherwise we'd have gotten reports or seen one of them. What if he runs into a hiker?"

"We'd better go after him. Make sure the trail is safe, in case anybody else is out here." She backed out from under the bushes, stowing the camera in her pack.

"Agreed. But no gunfire or else we'll scare them away before we can get back here with a team."

The sun was slipping behind Emory Peak as they worked their way carefully back down the ridge, keeping vigilant watch on the trail for any sign of the guard. Long shadows shrouded the wooded trail and each step over twigs and decaying leaves echoed too loudly off the silent trees.

Far off in the distance, something shrieked—a high-pitched scream, almost like that of a child. A shiver of fear skittered down Ashley's spine. She stopped, silently clutching Logan's hand.

Mountain lion. He mouthed the words.

It was getting close to dusk, wasn't it? The time predators came out. She took a couple of deep breaths, trying to slow her hammering heart. He squeezed her hand and released it, his fingers drifting toward his holster as he freed his other arm from its sling.

How much did mountain lions weigh? Enough to crush a person, she guessed. And then there were the claws. And the teeth.

This place was a long way from the streets of Washington, DC.

Breathe, she reminded herself. *Federal agents don't panic.* The canyon walls pressed in close on either side of the trees, and the darkness seemed to grow exponentially. Good thing she wasn't alone.

The path curved ahead, bending out of sight through a clump of trees. That one on the right, with the thick trunk, would be perfect for someone to hide behind, waiting.

Her fingers were on her gun before she realized it, nerves and instinct doing the decision-making. She pulled it out and released the safety, keeping it low and to the side, even though her conscious mind told her she was being paranoid.

Logan glanced back at her, shaking his head slightly. They'd agreed no gunfire. But his own fingers rested on the weapon in his holster.

The scream came again, louder this time. Exactly how long were a mountain lion's claws?

Only a few feet to go now to that bend.

A sudden flurry of motion in the bushes made Ashley swivel to the left, gun in front, as her heart leaped into her throat.

Two eyes gleamed up at her from beneath large ears in the growing twilight. A jackrabbit. Her breath came out in a ragged sort of laugh as it bolted across the path. She *was* being paranoid, but she wasn't used to dealing with criminals *and* wildlife.

Logan smirked, shaking his head at her. He walked forward again, passing the big tree without anything cataclysmic happening.

So much for all her hunches.

She let out a deep sigh as another sound from behind made her jump. From the right this time; probably the jackrabbit's cousin. She started to turn but something cold and hard jabbed into her side.

The muzzle of a gun.

"Drop it," the voice said. A man with a thick Spanish accent. Jimenez's guard.

SIXTEEN

Logan pulled his gun and spun around on the trail the moment he heard the man's voice. He inched back around the big tree until Ashley came into view. It was the same man they'd seen from the ridge, his rifle crammed into Ashley's ribs. Her jaw was clenched tight and both hands were up in the air, still clutching her gun.

"Freeze!" Logan ordered, aiming his weapon at the portion of the man's chest exposed on Ashley's right side. He was painfully aware how easily the man could shoot her before he could do anything about it. Beads of sweat formed on his forehead, but he kept his voice level. "I'm a law-enforcement ranger with the National Park Service. Put the gun down and back away from the lady. No one needs to get hurt."

The man shifted, moving further behind Ashley to use her as a shield. "Both of you, guns down. Now. Or I shoot her."

Logan gritted his teeth, trying to keep his heart from bursting out of his rib cage. Ashley's face was pale but her gaze was steely in the fading light. Silently, she mouthed the words, *Take the shot.* So much trust. His chest filled with warmth, even though his injured arm shook from the strain of keeping his gun steady.

He raised the gun to aim at the man's head, above Ashley's right shoulder. "You know we can't do that."

A loud scream rent the air—the mountain lion—so close even Logan started. Ashley's eyes went wide, the whites visible around her dark irises.

"¡Espíritu de Chisos!" the guard gasped. He glanced around at the dark woods, letting the rifle drop from Ashley's back.

All the chance she needed. She spun, shoving the rifle up and away from her body and aiming her own weapon at his torso. He reacted almost instantly, angling the muzzle out of her reach and slamming the butt of the rifle into her face before she could fire.

Logan lunged forward as she stumbled to the side, blood streaming from her nose. He drove his good shoulder into the man's stomach, sending the assault rifle flying and both of them crashing to the ground.

"Logan, the gun!" Ashley called, her voice muffled by the blood.

The man twisted and strained to reach the rifle, but Logan pushed off his chest and stretched as his injured shoulder screamed in protest. His fingertips found the strap and he flung the weapon backward out of reach. The man twisted again, trying to knock Logan off, but he pressed his knee down hard into the man's stomach.

"You're under arrest for assault." He pointed his gun at the man's chest, releasing one hand to get the cuffs from his belt.

"Logan…" Ashley's voice trembled.

"What?" he grunted, his injured shoulder arguing as his fingers closed around the cool metal of the cuffs.

A low growl came from the woods to his left. Very close.

The man pinned beneath his knee shook, muttering

what almost sounded like a prayer in Spanish. Logan followed his stare into the nearby trees.

A full-grown mountain lion, its eyes dancing like twin golden orbs, clung to one of the branches. The path lay easily within its forty-five-foot leaping ability.

Great. Logan's shoulders tensed. Maybe two dozen mountain lions lived in the eight hundred thousand acres making up this park, and one had to pick now to show up.

"Don't. Run." He emphasized each word. "Wave your arms and back away slowly."

The mountain lion growled again—more to announce its presence than to show aggression, he thought. He flipped the cuffs open, his gaze darting back and forth between the cougar and the paralyzed man beneath his knee.

Before Logan could get the cuffs around the man's wrists, he twisted, throwing Logan off balance and shoving him sideways. He crashed onto the path as the big cat snarled again. It shifted its weight on the branch, making the leaves swish and crackle.

"¡Espíritu!" the man cried out again, backing away from the mountain lion and Logan, his eyes wide.

"Don't run!" Logan scrambled to his feet, waving his arms. Mountain lions were shy of people, unless they felt threatened. Or were starving. This one held its ground.

Until the man took off down the path to the west in an all-out sprint.

The mountain lion coiled back on its haunches and, in one fluid motion, leaped onto the path ten feet away. In a heartbeat, it was gone, bolting after the fleeing man.

Logan gritted his teeth and lifted his gun toward the sky, firing three shots in quick succession. Hopefully enough to scare the big cat back into the woods. "Fool," he muttered through clenched teeth. "Never turn your back on a predator."

He'd call in the cougar sighting over the radio, and they'd have to get somebody out here to check the path for the man. Just in case.

Ashley touched his arm. "It wasn't your fault. Maybe he got away."

Her face was puffy and dark where the man had struck her, and blood crusted her nose and upper lip. He brushed a finger against her cheek. "Are you all right?"

"Fine." Her voice sounded muffled, like she was keeping in a big lump of tears. Always trying to prove herself.

"Come here." He slipped his hand around her back, tugging her into an embrace.

She buried her face in his shoulder, crying softly. After a few minutes she drew in a ragged breath. "I'm sorry."

"For what? Getting my shirt wet?" He laughed, and she laughed, too, mingled with the crying. He rubbed his hand up and down on her back, leaning his face against her hair. "I don't mind."

Far too intimate for coworkers, and yet… It felt right. In a different way than things ever had with Erin. Like they were in this thing together, not him trying to convince her to stay.

After a moment Ashley pulled back, blinking away the last of her tears. Breathtakingly beautiful despite the rapidly swelling cheek where she'd been hit. "My dad never wanted me to join the FBI. Said it was too dangerous. I always thought he meant criminals, not mountain lions."

Ah. That explained a few things. "Is that why you always have to prove yourself?"

"Probably." She wiped at her cheeks, taking a couple of deep breaths. "Time to get these photos back?"

He nodded. "Let's go catch the bad guys."

Night had fallen by the time they returned to Ashley's house and downloaded the pictures onto her laptop. Logan stuffed his aching arm back into the sling as they flipped through the images. The shots were good—several with clear, if small, views of the men's faces. Enough that Ashley thought she'd be able to run them through the FBI's database for possible matches.

The stars were out in full force as they walked past the quiet homes to headquarters, the white band of the Milky Way draped across the sky like a gauzy strip of fabric.

The lights were off, all the windows dark, as Logan unlocked the front door and let Ashley inside. They walked down the hall until they reached Logan's office.

"Whose light is that?" She pointed farther down the hall, where a soft glow emanated from beneath one of the doors.

"It's a conference room." One without an exterior window. Huh. He rubbed his chin. "I have no idea who would be in here this late on a Friday night." He let Ashley into his office. "You email Morton, I'm going to find out who it is."

"Be careful."

The hallway was silent as Logan tiptoed toward the conference room. The door was ajar and a hushed voice issued from the crack. He stopped beside the door, listening.

"No, I didn't get your message. I've been out all afternoon."

It sounded like…the superintendent? Why would he be here so late?

No response—must be on the phone. But why wasn't he using his own office?

"How do you know it was one of mine?" Barclay snapped.

Another pause as someone answered, and a sigh that sounded almost like he was in pain.

"I remember. I'll take care of it." With a noise loud enough to make Logan jump, Barclay slammed down the receiver. A chair scraped on the floor.

Logan retreated a handful of steps and approached the door again, this time making loud footsteps. There was no way to hide that he and Ashley were there, but at least he could pretend he hadn't heard Barclay's conversation.

This time only silence came from within as he knocked against the door, pushing it open enough to peek inside.

Barclay stood, leaning against a chair. His shoulders were slumped and there were dark circles under his eyes. Apparently under a lot of stress lately.

"Dr. Barclay? I saw the light. Just wondering who was working this late."

Barclay sighed. "Of course, Ranger Everett. I had to attend to a personal matter."

In the conference room? Probably better not to ask. But the gears turned in Logan's mind.

"I think I'll head home for the night." Barclay pulled away from the chair. One of his hands was wrapped in white bandaging.

Logan gestured at the injury. "What happened?"

The superintendent shifted his weight but offered a lopsided smile. Forced? "Slammed it in the car door. I broke three fingers. Pretty careless, huh?"

Very. Or was there another explanation? Logan hated

that his mind jumped immediately to the mole…but Barclay had never felt like the right fit for Big Bend.

They were getting closer to pinning Jimenez—was the broken hand a reminder of what Barclay had at stake?

"I hope it heals quickly."

Barclay walked over to the door and Logan moved aside for him as he flipped off the light and entered the hallway. "Why are *you* here so late?" He scanned Logan, his gaze lingering on the wrapped arm. "Didn't Chambers give you time off?"

"Yes, but I had a little work to catch up on." Guilt niggled at his insides at the stretched truth. Although, technically, it *was* park-related work that had him here now. "My trainee has taken up a lot of my time, so I'm getting behind on some of my regular tasks."

That was the truth. And apparently it appealed to Barclay's anger about the San Vicente incident, because he nodded. "Of course. I understand. Get some rest."

Logan stepped inside the office, his brows drawn in apparent concentration.

"Who was it?" Ashley glanced at him from over the top of her open laptop, curiosity pricking at her insides.

He sat in the chair opposite her—like a guest in his own office—and ran a hand through his hair. He waited, eyes on the door, as the echo of footsteps in the hallway receded. "Barclay."

"The superintendent?" Now that was a little unusual, wasn't it?

He nodded, pursing his lips. "And he had a few broken fingers."

"You don't suppose…?" Her mind leaped to the inevitable conclusion. He *had* been eager to get rid of her almost since the moment she'd arrived.

"Not gonna lie, the thought crossed my mind."

"Well…" She tapped a finger on her chin. "He knows who I am, which could explain how Jimenez's men knew my identity."

"And why they were breaking into your house right away." He rubbed his hand over his forehead. "But Ed Chambers knows your identity, too, doesn't he?"

"He does. But I don't think he's the guy."

Logan frowned. "What if we're letting personal feelings cloud our judgment?" He stood and began to pace. "Ed has a motive. His sister is sick, and I know they need money for her medical bills."

Ashley shook her head. "I've seen his personnel file. He's had nothing but a brilliant record of service. The case is stronger against Barclay. New to the park. Under visible stress. The file he gave me on Jimenez had almost nothing in it. And he's been against this investigation from the start."

Logan stopped pacing. "And there's the broken hand. But what's his motive?"

"Money? Maybe Ed knows more about his personal life."

"Maybe." Logan stared at the window for a moment, the inside of his office reflecting off the dark glass. "But did Barclay know we were going to San Vicente?"

She drummed her fingers on the desk. "Maybe Jimenez has men down there all the time and they recognized me from a photograph. Or they ID'd my contact and followed him."

"Then what about the map?" He sat, pointing at the yellowed paper on the desk. "Who sent it to you and how does Barclay know you have it?"

"Sam." The missing memory snapped into place with

beautiful clarity and Ashley slapped her hand down on the desk, scattering Logan's papers. "Sam sent it to me."

"You're sure? He never mentioned it to me."

"Absolutely sure. I remember now. I talked to him on the phone a few weeks before his death, and he told me he might've stumbled across something big. He said he was going to send me something." She could almost picture the way Sam must have looked as he'd talked to her, the way his eyes glowed when he was excited. "At the time, I figured he was talking about a new species of cactus or something, because he could get so animated about anything."

Logan grinned. "Sounds like Sam. Probably the most enthusiastic person I've ever met."

She leaned her chin against her hand, staring across the office for a moment, deep in thought. "But the question is…where did Sam get it?"

"What if he found it, say, in someone's office?"

"And then sent it to me? Why?"

He stood again, pointing at her as he spoke. "Because *you* are a federal agent. And if he suspected a mole within the park service, he wouldn't have known whom to trust. But he knew you could do something about it."

"And whoever he took it from must have figured, or even suspected, that I had it."

"He was friends with Will Sykes. I wonder if he told Will about the map."

Ashley chewed the inside of her lip. "Maybe. How can I find out without telling him who I am?"

"You can't. But we'll think of something. What about that first day you were here? Why did you go to Santa Elena, and who knew about it?"

It always came back to that one day still missing from her mind. She blew out an exasperated sigh. "I wish I could remember. I've got almost everything back, except for those twenty-four hours. All I know is I went to sleep in my apartment in DC, and I woke up in the Rio Grande."

"Nothing in the middle? Not even a clue?"

"Believe me, I've tried." She tapped a finger against her chin, trying to catch the elusive idea fluttering through her mind. "Where did you say you...found Sam?" So hard to ask without letting her voice crack.

"Dodson Trail—the outer rim." He showed her on a park map. "About here. Why?"

"I wonder... Maybe I wanted to drive past the trail. Surely the park service must've told us where he was found. You don't suppose his death could be linked to Jimenez, do you?"

"Maybe." Logan's brow furrowed. "But he wasn't found anywhere near the mine. As much as I want it to not be my fault."

She leveled her gaze at him, wishing there was some way to wipe the regret from his features. "It wasn't your fault, Logan. Either way."

"But how did you end up at Santa Elena if you were only driving to the trailhead?"

Ashley shrugged. "Who knows? Curiosity? A lead I was following on Jimenez?"

"Well, it doesn't matter. We can still solve this case." He resumed pacing, as if the movement helped his thoughts. It only took him three strides in each direction to cross the room. Every muscle in his upper body was taut, alert, despite the arm in the sling. She couldn't have hand-picked a better partner.

Her heart twisted. Her job here was almost done. And even though she knew *something* was happening between them, she didn't know what it meant. Or if either of them would be willing to act on it. A relationship between the two of them would be doomed from the start, wouldn't it?

Her computer chimed—a response from her boss at the FBI. "Morton got back to me."

"And?"

She scanned the message. "All three men can be positively identified as working for Jimenez. And—" she re-read the last few sentences just to make sure "—he gave me the green light to arrest them."

Logan froze, his eyes sparking with energy as they flicked to meet Ashley's gaze.

She rounded the desk and flung her arms around his neck, being careful of his injured shoulder. "We did it."

He slipped his arm around her back, holding her tightly. "We sure did."

She pulled back, gazing up at him, her breath catching at the way the light shifted in his green eyes, from excitement to something more subdued. Cautious. Questioning. The ache of past hurt lingered there beneath the surface and she longed to soothe it away.

He tipped his chin lower, closer, and without giving herself time to second-guess, she stretched to press her lips to his mouth. He kissed her back, threatening to make her heart burst from sheer joy. It was like coming home, to a place she'd been missing her whole life. Finally something made sense amid the heartache and confusion and fear of the last week.

If only it could last. But their lives were in two different places, and she wasn't naïve enough to think one kiss meant forever. They were only making things harder.

Placing both hands on his cheeks, she pulled away. Swallowed. "I… I'm sorry. I have no right to—" She broke off, shaking her head. *Stupid.* He'd already had his heart broken once. "After we arrest Jimenez and the case is over, I have to—"

"It's okay, Ashley." He clasped one of her hands, pressing it to his lips. "I know. You don't have to say it. I won't kiss you again." His lips tipped into a crooked grin. "Unless you ask."

He released her hand, leaving her breathless and confused. Did he *want* her to stay in Big Bend? Would she, if he asked?

"Thanks," she mumbled, gnawing at the inside of her lip. She'd worked her whole life to get to this point in her career, never questioning the sacrifices. But now? She wasn't so sure.

Logan cleared his throat. "What about the inside man? We'll never catch him."

Back to business. Time to stuff her heart in a drawer and ignore its protests. "I know. But the Bureau or the federal prosecutor might be able to get it out of Jimenez later."

"Plea bargain?"

"Let's hope it doesn't come to that." Maybe whoever it was would slip up during the arrest.

Logan resumed his pacing, rubbing his hand against his jaw. "How do we pull this off without the mole tipping off Jimenez?"

"We'll call in an FBI team from the local office in El Paso."

"You know that's five hours away, right?"

"Yes, I know. But we have to figure out the right timing anyway. If we arrive when Jimenez isn't there, we'll scare him off." She rubbed her eyes, suddenly exhausted by all the logistics that had seemed exciting only minutes ago. "Here's what I think. Since we believe they might be transporting the gold at night, our best bet would be to reach the mine at midday. That will give Jimenez's crew time to get involved with their work, and hopefully give us the element of surprise."

"Agreed." He hesitated, adding, "How do we keep something like this secret from our rangers?"

"I'll tell the agents to meet us at the trailhead. It won't be a big team. They should be able to slip under the radar."

"What about Ed? If we bring him in on the raid, he can help with the cover-up."

Ashley nodded. It made sense. They trusted him, and he could ensure whoever was assigned to patrol the trailhead wasn't there at midday. "And it'll be good to have another person who knows this terrain."

"Barclay is going to hate this when he finds out." Logan's mouth tipped into a crooked smile as he ran a hand through his sandy-brown hair, making the ends stand out at odd angles. He looked almost boyish for a moment, but she knew a warrior's heart beat in his chest.

Even with everything that had happened, she'd never regret coming here and meeting him.

"Yeah, he will." She smiled. "Even if he's innocent."

Between Morton's advance communication and Ashley's call to the El Paso office, it didn't take long to arrange for a small team of agents to meet them at the Pine Canyon trailhead the next day.

When she hung up the phone, Logan nodded toward the door. "Come on, it's late. Let me walk you home. We can finalize plans in the morning."

They followed the familiar path to her house in silence and Ashley stopped in front of her door. His face was visible in the soft glow of the moonlight. Strong chin. Warm eyes. And his lips… Well, she didn't need to remember what they felt like.

"Thank you. For everything. I couldn't have done this without you."

He smiled, joy and sorrow mingling. His voice was low and rough when he spoke. "It's been my pleasure."

She rested her fingertips lightly on his chest. "Good night, Logan."

"Good night, Ashley."

It took a long, long time to fall asleep.

SEVENTEEN

The day dawned hot and muggy, with hazy wisps of clouds hovering on the edges of a dull blue, faded-denim sky. Ashley woke early—too early to expect Logan. But there was no way she could fall back to sleep, not with the day looming ahead.

She tried to roll some of the tension out of her shoulders, shifting restlessly on the edge of her bed. Why the sudden nerves? Maybe because she still didn't know who the traitor was. Or maybe it was because the day looked sultry and miserable, and she'd hoped for a more auspicious beginning.

Whatever the case, maybe a jog around the neighborhood would clear away the jitters. It only took a few minutes to pull on a pair of black yoga pants and a running top. She left her gun in its place under the extra pillow and the map tucked between the mattress and box spring, along with her computer. She'd just finished quaffing a large glass of water when someone knocked at the door.

"Logan, you're early—" She stopped short as she opened the door. Not Logan. "Oh, hey, Will. What's up?" Perhaps a golden opportunity to see what he knew about Sam.

He shifted his weight from one foot to the other and

leaned one forearm against her doorjamb, somehow managing to look both suave and nervous at the same time. "Hey, got a minute? I'm heading out on patrol, but I wanted to talk to you. It'll be quick."

"Sure." She opened the door. As he passed by her, Ashley caught a sudden whiff of that same soap she had noticed at the staff picnic. So familiar—hauntingly familiar—but the connection dangled there on the edge of her brain, just out of reach.

"What happened to your face?" He gestured at her bruised cheek, which didn't look a whole lot better this morning. His dark eyes were full of concern. "Did that happen in San Vicente?"

"Oh, um, n-no," she stammered, grasping for a reasonable explanation that didn't involve telling the truth. "I ran into some trouble out on the trail yesterday. But I'll tell you about it some other time. Want to sit?"

"No time. I wanted to see how you were doing. It's a big adjustment, moving here, and now with all these scary things that keep happening to you…" He let the words trail away, fidgeting with a button on his cuff.

"That's so kind of you, Will." Ashley smiled, trying to set him at ease. There had to be some way to steer this conversation toward his friendship with Sam. But how? "You know, there was something I wanted to ask you. I heard a rumor about a ranger dying here recently. Is it true?" She shifted her weight back and forth, feigning nervousness. "I'm a little hesitant to ask Logan. He seems kind of secretive about it."

An outright lie. *Sorry, Logan.* She was pretty sure he'd understand.

Will ran his hand through his thick, dark hair, a gesture that reminded her of Logan. But along with the motion came that scent of fabric softener, demanding her attention. "Um, yeah. It was pretty tragic."

Ashley heard the words, saw his lips moving, but her mind suddenly filled with recognition so forceful she had to swallow back the bile rising into her esophagus.

Will was the one who had dumped her into the river.

Images flashed through her mind, one after another, filling the last blank place in her memory. She had driven down past the trail where Sam had died, and then, with nothing else to do but grieve, she had kept going all the way to the end of the road. Right to the Santa Elena Canyon parking lot, where she had inadvertently stumbled across a drug exchange.

She remembered the blow to the head, the distant sound of voices and the feel of someone stuffing her gun into her pocket. And the smell—that fabric softener—on the man's shirt as he'd lugged her limp body to the river.

Well, Sykes, one of the others had said, *you're in for it now. She looks like law enforcement. How are we going to cover up this mess?*

Don't tell my uncle.

Will had panicked. He had picked her up, carried her to the Rio Grande and thrown her in.

And he had gone out of his way to be friendly to her ever since, because he wanted to know what she remembered.

That truck that had run her and Logan off the road on the way to Terlingua? It was probably whomever had picked up the drugs on this side of the river.

"Ashley, what's wrong?" Will's words snapped her back to the present, where they both stood inside her house. With the door shut. And Will's back leaning against it.

"Nothing." She forced a smile even though her head

was spinning. She had to tell Logan—if Barclay *was* one of Jimenez's men, he wasn't alone. Will, so deceptively charming, was a mole, too. It took all her self-control to keep her hands from shaking. "Just sad. For the family. Of the ranger that died."

Her gun—it was in the bedroom, under the pillow. How long would it take to reach it? Should she try taking him down now, before he realized she had remembered the truth?

"You know…" Her voice came out a half octave too high. "I've got some things to take care of, and I'm sure you need to get going. We can talk more later."

Her stomach turned over as she waited, hoping he couldn't read the visceral terror on her face.

"Of course." Will's lips curled into a smile, but his eyes filled with something else that looked a lot like… fear.

She took a step back, letting out the breath she'd been holding as he turned for the door.

Before she could react, he lunged. Black flashed in his hand and the gun smashed into the side of her head, filling her vision with stars as her legs crumpled. The last thing she heard before she blacked out was Will's voice.

"I'm sorry, Ashley. I didn't want it to end like this. Not for you and not for Sam."

Ashley was gone. Logan pounded on her door as Ed waited with him on the front step, but nobody answered. All the hairs stood up on his arms.

He strode over to her window and peered into the living area. Empty. Tension roiled in his stomach. With a glance at Ed, he walked around the back to the bedroom window.

Nothing.

Wait! The sash was open an inch. And on the ground—footprints. At least two sets.

"Ed!"

The chief ranger dashed around to the back and examined his find. "Too big for Ashley's?"

"They're not hers," Logan managed to choke out. *Failed.* He'd failed. The world collapsed in on him as he imagined her tied up, gagged, maybe dead.

Please, Lord, not that… The prayer ripped its way out of his soul.

Ed grasped his shoulders. "We're going to find her. You and me. Okay, buddy?"

He nodded woodenly, digging cold fingertips into his hair, and walked with Ed around to the front.

The door was unlocked, no sign of a struggle inside. Except… He dropped to one knee, examining the white linoleum tiles in the entryway, where a few red splotches had almost escaped his attention. Some of the blood came away on one of his fingers. "Happened this morning."

Ed nodded grimly.

It didn't take long to search the small home. In her bedroom, Ed lifted one of the pillows to reveal Ashley's gun.

Logan pursed his lips. "She must've let whoever it was in."

"Or forgot to lock her door."

No, it had to have been the mole. Somebody she trusted enough to let inside her house. But who? Surely not Barclay, not after last night's conversation. Somebody else they'd overlooked?

Thinking about it wasn't going to get Ashley back. "We have to assume Jimenez has her and take the team in to the mine."

"Agreed."

The next two hours passed in a brutally slow haze of anxiety and preparation. Logan notified the FBI team of Ashley's capture and arranged for them to put a helicopter in the air as soon as the raid was finished. Just in case she wasn't there.

Logan and Ed were already waiting at the Pine Canyon trailhead when the team of agents arrived. Six agents, wearing FBI windbreakers over body armor, climbed out of two vehicles. Logan spread a trail map out on the hood of one of the cars and went over the details of the raid.

Fifteen minutes later Ed led two agents in first to clear the trail of guards. They only found one and, mercifully, no evidence of anyone being mauled by a mountain lion the previous night.

Once the guard was secured, Logan signaled his team. One agent stayed on the trail to cover their backs and the rest scrambled in behind Logan up the steep mountainside. His legs burned from the extra weight of his Kevlar flak jacket and gear, but he barely noticed as he prayed for Ashley's safety. She *had* to be in there.

The mine entrance, hidden in a cleft of rock behind a cover of bushes, stayed quiet as they approached. To avoid direct observation, Logan led the team in from above, positioning them around the mine entrance. A guard sounded the alarm, opening fire.

"Stop!" Ed called out from behind the protection of a large boulder. "This is National Park Service law enforcement and the FBI. Cease fire or we'll shoot."

When the man ignored him, Ed signaled to the agent who'd claimed to be their best shot. The man nodded, braced his gun against a rock and took the guard down.

Logan dropped into the cleft from above, followed by one of the agents, who secured the fallen guard. When the others were in position, he stepped inside the mine, gun up, flashlight on.

Pale faces blinked at him from within the darkness. A few lanterns glowed in the background, casting dark shadows from the occupants on the glittering walls.

"Freeze!" he ordered, though no one had moved. Most of them held tools—a jackhammer, a shovel, an old-school pickax like something out of a Western movie.

Sudden movement to his side sent his heart into his throat, but another agent was ready. "Drop it."

The man's face, illuminated in a flashlight beam, was familiar. José, from San Vicente. He scowled but dropped his gun with a heavy clatter to the cave floor. Only one other man was armed. The rest, unfortunate souls, had been carted in solely for the purpose of manual labor.

"Amazing." Ed shone his light around the inside of the mine. Narrow veins of white and yellow quartz, most of them already partially removed, ran through the hard rock wall.

Logan traced his fingers along one of the rough veins where someone had recently been working. Tiny gold flecks glinted in the quartz. Gold in Big Bend, right there beneath his fingertips. Ashley had been right.

But she wasn't here.

They'd cuffed everyone they'd found and searched the mine, which ran back in a single tunnel that grew narrower and narrower to the point of claustrophobia before it ended. Three guards in total, plus six workers. No Jimenez and no Ashley. The other two men from San Vicente weren't there, either.

Logan stalked out the mine entrance and scrambled back down the hill to the trail, where the agents had hauled the suspects. He found José. "Where's Jimenez?"

"No hablo inglés." José shrugged.

Logan stepped closer, his face inches away. "You can either cooperate, or I can make the next few days very difficult for you."

José smirked. "You're not allowed to hurt me."

Without hesitating, Logan crushed his knuckles into the man's mouth. "Try me."

"Logan!" Ed called, eyebrows raised.

But Logan ignored him. Time was slipping away and every passing moment increased the odds of Jimenez and Ashley disappearing across the border where he would never find them again. Too many hours had passed already.

José turned to the side, spitting out a mouthful of blood. "He's not here."

"That's obvious," Logan growled. "Where is he? And the woman?"

"The federal agent?" José laughed. "Dead by now."

A knife in the stomach would've felt better, but Logan clenched his jaw and sucked in a deep breath. Maybe he was telling the truth, maybe not. In either case, José had known exactly whom he was talking about. Did that mean she'd been there?

Movement behind José caught his eye. One of the forced laborers. He raised a wavering left hand. The fingertips were filthy and ragged, and multiple scrapes covered his knuckles. Poor man.

Logan strode over to him. "Do you speak English?"

"A little." The man nodded, glancing nervously at José.

"You're free. He can't hurt you anymore," Logan assured him. "Have you seen an American woman? Brown hair?" He held up a hand. "This tall?"

When the man nodded again, Logan's breath lodged in his lungs. Ashley *had* been here.

"When?" he prompted.

"Today. Gone now. Jimenez take her." The man pointed to the west, where the trail dwindled away into a wall of thick brush. "That way. We go that way with gold, too. Trucks wait on road."

Just as Ashley's contact had told her, they were getting the gold out through Juniper Canyon. He could see now where the foliage had been damaged and cut at the trail's end, leaving a narrow, barely visible path.

"Where's he taking her?" Logan balled his fists, every nerve in his body waiting impatiently for the answer. "To Mexico?"

"No. To desert. Kill her."

No. His fingernails dug into his palms as he turned to find Ed already beside him. "I'm taking two agents into Juniper Canyon. Will's checking campsites on Glenn Spring Road. He can help search."

"I'll get that FBI chopper up over the stretch between Juniper and Mariscal." Ed squeezed Logan's shoulder, his voice steady as always. "Go get her."

Ashley's head throbbed. Again. She groaned, forcing her eyes open. The sun scorched down like an oven set to broil.

"Good, she's awake." Someone kicked her hard in the ribs. Not Will's voice, but the face was invisible against the bright yellow orb of sun overhead.

Another voice—a man's, crisp and clear but with an accent—said, "Manuel, stop kicking the federal agent. Stand her up."

Ah, one of her friends from San Vicente. Lovely. He yanked her to her feet, making her head spin like a top. A black SUV and a beat-up truck were parked nearby, off to the side of the dirt road where they now stood. Her hands were bound tightly behind her back and a rock dug into her foot.

Great. No shoes. She'd never had the chance to put them on. Logan would have a thing or two to say about that…if she ever saw him again.

She was still in her running clothes, which meant she had nothing. No gun, no cell phone, no water, no knife. No way to tell Logan what had happened, or where to find her, or that he had to arrest Will Sykes.

A man dressed in a linen shirt and khaki pants stood a few feet away. "We meet at last, Agent Thompson."

"Jimenez?" she asked, although it was hardly necessary. Despite his short stature, he wore the air of a man used to getting his way.

He nodded.

She glanced around, trying to orient herself. The Chisos towered behind her, close enough she was still on the US side. But the profile of the mountains didn't match the view from the mine and the cactuses and low brush of the open desert surrounded them. They must be somewhere in that long barren stretch between the mine and the border. "What do you want with me?"

"We've known who you are since your second day in this park. You don't think I can let you keep chasing me, do you?"

Second day? That would explain the almost immediate break-in at her home. "Will?" She faltered. How could he have known? "Did Barclay tell him?"

"The superintendent?" Jimenez laughed. "No, my nephew knew the moment he met you."

"Nephew?" She shook her head, trying to clear away the cobwebs. "He's only got one relative listed on his record, and it isn't an uncle."

"His mother is my sister." Jimenez smirked. "Naturally, I wouldn't want his record tarnished by association. Easy enough to change, with the right influence."

She scrunched her eyebrows together. So hot out here. Her mouth already felt pasty dry. "But how did he recognize—" She stopped short.

Of course. The variable she'd always known was possible but hadn't expected. "Sam showed him my picture, didn't he?" He must've been very close to Will. Maybe even wanted to set her up with him one day. She shook her head.

"Yes. It was a coincidence he had the chance to kill you on your first night. Unfortunately he didn't realize it was you until the next day, when he got a good look at your face. A shame he didn't take a closer look the first time around. But, no matter, we will finish the job soon." The cold glint in his eyes sent a shiver down Ashley's spine.

She had to stall, to give Logan time to find her. Ignoring the fear clawing at her heart, she took a steadying breath. "What about the map? How did you know I had it?"

"The logical conclusion. After my careless nephew lost his copy, your brother found the mine. When you showed up, the best explanation was that he had sent the map to you."

Sam had found the mine. Her heart broke. Why had he gone searching alone? Impulsive, overconfident, energetic Sam. "And his death…?"

"Not an accident. Very good, Agent Thompson. Shooting him would have been too obvious, so we left him to die of exposure." He shrugged. *No loss.*

Her insides burned. The man who had killed her brother stood three feet away and here she was, unable to do anything about it.

Where was God's perfect justice? *How long, oh Lord, will You wait?*

"They'll find you," she snapped, "and you'll spend a lifetime in jail for all the people you've hurt."

He laughed again. "I think not. In fact, before you join your brother, I wanted to show you something." He raised a hand toward one of the vehicles and two men got out, one with his hands behind his back.

Her stomach tightened. It was her contact from San Vicente.

"Recognize him?" Jimenez asked softly. Dangerously. "He won't be feeding tips to the FBI anymore." He pulled a handgun from his belt as the guard forced the man to his knees on the hot, dusty road.

The man on the ground wept, tears running down his wrinkled cheeks, but he kept his back straight. *"Para mi Lena."*

Jimenez placed the barrel of the gun against the man's forehead. "This is your fault, Agent Thompson."

Ashley opened her mouth to object, or to beg—she wasn't sure which—but before any sound came out, Jimenez pulled the trigger.

Her eyes snapped shut as the man's blood splattered across her face. Bile burned in her esophagus.

It would be her turn next. She clenched her jaw, staring at Jimenez. Logan would catch him and bring him to justice. "They'll find you."

"But they won't find you," he jeered. "Not alive, anyway."

Unshed tears burned in Ashley's eyes as she waited to be forced to her knees. To feel the cold metal ring of the barrel dig into her skin.

Instead, at a nod from Jimenez, Manuel and the other man dragged her toward the truck.

"Goodbye, Agent Thompson," Jimenez called after her. "Please give my best to your brother."

Her stomach dropped. They were going to dump her in the desert, right there on Dodson Trail, like they had done with Sam. And Logan would have no idea where to look.

She didn't know which hurt more—the thought of never seeing him again or knowing he would blame himself for her death.

EIGHTEEN

Logan crouched behind a rock formation at the trailhead of Juniper Canyon, watching the two parked vehicles fifty yards away on the dirt road that led south. He and the two agents had taken the narrow, rugged path—created by Jimenez—across the ridge from Pine Canyon Trail to Juniper Canyon, and then followed the steep descent through the canyon to the base of the mountains.

Here they were in the Sierra Quemada, the burnt lands, where the only cover came in the form of rocks and barrel cactuses. Moments before, when a gunshot catapulted his heart into his throat, Logan had crept as close as he could without risking being seen. The other two agents had split to either side.

The truck engine roared to life. They couldn't afford to wait, not if Ashley was in one of those vehicles. The way the SUV was parked blocked his view of the people, but there were at least two, maybe three, sets of boots visible beneath the vehicle. And what looked like the victim of the gunshot.

He couldn't stop to consider the possibilities.

He dashed forward, keeping low to the ground, moving from barrel cactus to cactus, until he finally reached the back right bumper of the SUV. Doors slammed, and the truck sped away, kicking up a cloud of dust on the dirt road.

Voices came from the far side of the SUV, speaking rapidly in Spanish. Logan crouched low, peered beneath the vehicle and watched as a pair of hands hoisted a body.

Not Ashley. Relief threatened to make his legs go weak.

As the man with the body headed for the SUV, Logan slipped along the far side. A faint pulsing reached his ears from across the desert to the west—the helicopter.

He edged around to the front of the SUV as the latch clicked to open the rear tailgate.

The other man had stopped beside the driver's-side door.

Leading with his gun, Logan swiveled around the bumper and aimed his gun at a well-dressed man who could only be Jimenez. "National Park Service. Drop your weapon."

Jimenez's eyes widened for a second before his face contorted into a smile.

"Drop it," Logan repeated. "Or I *will* shoot."

Jimenez held up his handgun, dropping it onto the sand. "No, you won't. You Americans are all the same. So worried about protecting everyone's rights. Trials and justice and law."

"Instead of the anarchy you want?"

"It's not anarchy." He smirked. "I'm merely helping the government. Offering employment. And justice."

The other man appeared from behind the vehicle—Manuel, from San Vicente—his gun pointed at Logan. Not more than ten feet away. Hard to miss at that range.

Logan didn't flinch, even though every nerve in his body begged for self-preservation. "Drop the weapon, Manuel."

Manuel ignored him, taking a step forward.

"Last chance, Manuel," Logan said through gritted teeth. "FBI agents are in position. You're not getting out of here."

Manuel's gaze darted back and forth, his knuckles white around the gun. But Jimenez's eyes narrowed, his lips parting to give the order to fire.

Before any sound came out, the two agents stepped up behind Manuel. "Freeze."

Manuel's eyes went wide, nostrils flaring.

Logan sensed his panic, the way his finger hovered over the trigger despite the agents behind him. Instinct told him to move and he flung himself sideways, rolling across the hard dirt as bullets from Manuel's gun raked the sand where he'd been standing a split second before.

Another shot fired and Manuel crumpled to the ground.

Jimenez's face paled, but he clenched his teeth together. "I'll repay you for this."

"I don't think so." Logan climbed to his feet, pulling out his handcuffs. "Not where you're going."

While the agents secured the two suspects, Logan radioed in their position. Precious minutes had passed since the truck had driven away. Had Ashley been inside it? Or had they taken her somewhere else entirely?

Questioning Jimenez was useless.

Logan would need that chopper, a dark speck growing larger on the horizon.

Ed's voice crackled over the radio. "Sykes will be at your position in five minutes to help search."

Ashley sank to the ground beside a barrel cactus, narrowly avoiding the giant spines. Everything around her was brown, brittle, dry. Or spikey. Dead, crunchy grasses. Brown brush that wouldn't sprout leaves until the next rain. Leathery succulents hoarding their toxic alkaloid water beneath a thousand spikes.

The Chisos loomed to the north, Emory Peak visible against the bright blue sky. To the southwest lay the smaller outlying mountains. Somewhere in between ran Dodson Trail, the one tiny thread of hope she had, because at the end of its twelve-mile length lay a paved parking lot and a water cache.

The other option was to go back. They'd blindfolded her before dumping her out here, but the dirt road where she'd seen Jimenez was probably only a few miles away. No water that way, though, unless rangers were searching the area.

She turned over one of her feet, prodding gently at the red, bubbling blisters and pulling out a sharp spine. At least they'd had the decency to cut her hands free.

Sweat dripped down her back, down her neck, down over her eyebrows. Soaking even her sweat-wicking workout gear. She'd laugh if it wasn't so much effort.

Logan had taught her all about desert survival and the signs of heat stroke. Muscle cramps would start soon. Her arms and face were already red, both from her internal heat and from sun exposure. But the real danger wouldn't begin until she stopped sweating. When her body ran out of moisture reserves and her internal temperature would rise unchecked.

Ashley shuddered. Better to think about survival than death.

First rule of desert survival: don't panic. *Check.* FBI training had taught her to stay calm in any situation.

Second rule: find cover. Shade wasn't an option. She'd considered ripping off part of her shirt to make a hat of sorts but decided stretchy black fabric over one's head probably wouldn't make a big dent on things.

Third rule: conserve water. Breathing with her mouth shut was about the extent of things. Logan had cleared up the cactus misconception on the first day. Those big, old barrel cactuses weren't full of water, they were full of alkaloid toxins that would send the unwary backpacker into a downward spiral of gut-emptying vomiting and diarrhea. A few varieties, like the prickly pear, were edible, but how exactly did one get into a cactus with nothing but bare hands? A sharp rock might do the job…if it came to that.

She'd keep an eye out for any young prickly pear pads, or *nopales*, as she walked. Or a tinaja. Maybe there'd be a bit of collected water left from the rainfall earlier in the week.

Her limbs felt like lead weights as she hauled herself to her feet. Maybe it was better to sit still in the hot sun than to walk in it, but surely there was shade somewhere out here. Surely, if she pressed on a little bit longer, she'd find the trail. Maybe with hikers.

Sam had thought the same thing, hadn't he? He'd almost made it to the trail. A half mile away, Logan had said.

Was Sam's skin this red already?

Did his tongue cling to the roof of his mouth the way Ashley's did? Like a cotton ball ready to choke her.

Why did the good people have to die, while the bad guys drove away in their air-conditioned trucks with bags full of gold?

Didn't God care?

Useless anger tore at her insides. The same question had plagued her since Sam's death. Her brother had loved God. Trusted Him.

She had loved and trusted Him, too. And what had He done for them?

She stopped short as a picture forced its way into her mind, into her heart, so abruptly her breath caught.

Jesus, a crown of thorns on his head. Nails in his hands. A spear thrust into his side. Crying out as he bore the sins of the world, taking the punishment each one of them deserved. God made flesh.

God had done *that* for her and Sam.

And all she could do was complain. She sank to her knees on the hot, rocky ground, hardly able to breathe, and pressed a trembling hand to her mouth.

I'm sorry. Her esophagus burned, but no tears came. No water to spare. *I'm so, so sorry for doubting You.*

Her anger melted away like snow in the face of His love and, finally, His peace—the peace that passed all understanding—flowed into the brittle hole she had guarded for so long inside her chest.

A little tinaja filled with living water.

But whosoever drinketh of the water that I shall give him shall never thirst.

She smiled. Sam had that water. He was with Jesus now. Waiting for her.

The thought reverberated in her chest as she struggled to her feet. She'd get to see him soon, and she could tell him she finally understood about Jimenez and the map and what had happened. She could even understand why he loved this place. Vast, dangerous, wild…but free. The constraints of the city, the noise of everyday life that prevented her from really thinking and feeling—they were all gone. Out here, in air so fresh it was like no one else had ever breathed it, nothing stood between her and the things that mattered. Like knowing her Savior.

And acknowledging all those feelings she'd tried so hard to avoid. Grief for Sam. Anger at God. Love for...

Ashley tried to stop his name from forming in her mind, but she was too weary to fight anymore. The words rolled around in her head and in her heart, unwilling to be contained any longer. She was in love with Logan. It didn't make sense—she'd known him such a short time, and she'd never see him again—but there it was. She loved him.

There were so many things she would have liked to tell him.

The trail of footprints was fading away as the wind shifted. Logan jogged after them, ignoring the sweat beading on his forehead. Ignoring the way his heart hammered in his chest each time he passed another plant to look behind.

Exactly as it had been when he'd searched for Sam, only that time it had been too late. Vultures had circled overhead then; their dark shapes blotted the blue sky now. He could hardly breathe as he imagined what might be beneath them. He wasn't sure he could handle it if he found her like that. Especially not when there was so much bound up in his heart he hadn't told her. Ashley needed to know how he felt about her... How much he cared about her—no, *loved* her—despite all his efforts not to.

Please, Lord, please...

He scarcely noticed the pack rubbing against his back, holding two precious containers of water. Will was coming right behind him with the radio. They would call her location in to the chopper as soon as they found her. Airlift her to safety.

How much farther could she have gone? He and Will

had followed the pickup's tracks and Ashley's prints as far into the desert as they could. When they'd had to stop driving, Logan had tumbled out to continue on foot, Will only a few minutes behind as he called in their location and gathered more supplies from the NPS truck.

The thought squirmed in the back of his mind that maybe he had missed her. Walked right on past. Ashley was strong, but nobody was strong enough to walk for miles in this heat without water. At some point, she'd have to stop, even without shade.

He called her name again, as he had done every minute for the past fifteen. Always willing her to answer, always hearing nothing but the wind and the sound of his own footsteps.

This time, though, he heard something else. He stopped, heart lodging in his throat, listening.

"Ashley!" he called again.

Rustling nearby.

He spun toward a waist-high prickly pear cactus a short distance to his left. And then he saw it. A pile of brown hair, dark against the sand. *Ashley*. He covered the space between them in a heartbeat, throwing himself to his knees beside her, his breath—no, his life—on hold as he slipped his fingers against her burning red throat to feel for a pulse.

Alive. Praise God, *she was alive*. He wasn't too late.

NINETEEN

Somewhere through her haze of utter exhaustion, Ashley felt a hand slide under the back of her head. Cold wetness ran along her bloody, chapped lips and down her chin. A little trickle made it into her mouth—sweet like sugar—and she opened her mouth wider, desperate for more.

"Easy. Just a little at a time or you'll throw it back up."

Logan. She pried her eyelids open, taking in his tanned face, defined jaw and the way his hair ruffled in the wind. Had to be her imagination. Maybe she was delirious, sucking down sand. But the strong arm under her—she didn't think her mind could come up with that, too.

"Chopper'll be here soon. Hang in there for me, okay?" The tender, aching tone to his words tore at Ashley's heart. He glanced away. "Over here, Will! I found her!"

Wait. Fear pulsed through her veins. *No, not Will.* Logan didn't know. She wanted to shake her head but her muscles wouldn't work.

Logan smiled. "It's okay. We've got you now. You're safe."

Why didn't he understand? She moved her lips but

her desiccated brick of a tongue refused to move. Logan gave her more of the precious water, stroking her hair with his hand, not knowing whom he had called over.

She groaned, struggling to lift her head. May as well be a cannonball attached to her shoulders.

"Easy." Logan glanced over his shoulder.

"Will…" she rasped.

"He'll be here in a minute." His brows drew together. "What is it?"

Too late. A man stepped into view behind Logan, his dark hair and tanned face immediately recognizable in the blinding sunlight. One hand dangled at his side, the other was behind his back.

"Did you find her?" Will's voice was choked with anxiety. "Is she alive?"

"Yeah." Logan grinned. "She'll make it, but we need to call in a medevac now."

"I was afraid of that." Will's voice was cold and sterile as he pulled his hand out from behind his back, sunlight flashing off his gun. "Hands up, Logan."

No. Ashley mouthed the word, but no sound came out. Will's eyes had a haunted, half-wild look that removed any doubt he would fire. But the small mouthfuls of water Logan had given her? They were working into her body, replenishing the shriveling cells.

She couldn't speak; she certainly couldn't stand. But maybe, just maybe, she could reach Logan's gun where it rested in the holster at his waist.

The color drained from Logan's face. His lips parted as if he wanted to say something, but he stayed silent. Slowly he raised his hands, never taking his eyes off her.

She glanced at his gun, so rapidly she wasn't sure Logan would catch the flash of her eyes. He froze, staring at her for a fraction of a second, almost as if he was deliberating whether it was worth the risk. He nodded, his mouth forming a grim line.

"It was you, wasn't it?" Logan asked Will, trying to buy them time as the strength trickled back into her limbs. "You were the one helping Jimenez smuggle drugs in and gold out."

"Yes." Will frowned. "And no one would have figured it out, if she had gone back home before she remembered everything."

"Remembered what, Will?" Logan's voice was calm, almost soothing—meant to keep him talking.

Ashley slid her hand across her stomach, toward the gun.

"I…" Will's voice cracked and he sucked in a ragged breath. When he spoke again, the words came out emotionless once more. "She showed up at an exchange—surprised us. It was dark and I didn't recognize her. Not until I'd already knocked her out. Then…I panicked."

"You threw her in the river?" Logan's tone was still calm but strained with concealed rage beneath the words.

"When she…when she showed up at work as a new ranger, I thought it was over. But she didn't recognize me, didn't remember." Will's voice trembled as the emotion leaked back into it. "But my uncle wanted—"

"Your uncle?" Logan interrupted, his eyes widening with the realization. "Jimenez?"

Will nodded miserably. "My mother's brother. She tried to hide us from him, but after my father died…I had to work for him, to protect my family. He wanted me to watch Ashley and to get back that stupid map. Sam was my friend. You have to believe me." His eyes begged them to understand. "When she remembered what happened, I had to turn her over. And now that she's still not dead…I have no choice."

"You do have a choice." Logan's voice was both authoritative and soothing. "You can still make the right decision. We can all walk out of here together."

Will shook his head, his face contorted into a grimace. "I can't spend my life in jail. No one else will take care of my mother and my sister."

"What do you think will happen if you return without us?"

His eyes grew hard. "I think they'll believe me. Before we could find Ashley, one of Jimenez's men caught us. You were shot and left for dead. I barely escaped. Of course, I'll have to drag your body a fair way from here, but I'm sure I can manage."

"Will—"

"Enough talking!" Will snapped, waving the gun at Logan. "Toss me your gun and back away from her. There's no reason for her to see this."

Will hadn't even looked at her—as if he didn't dare risk eye contact with the woman he kept trying to kill.

Ashley's arm dropped down against the hot sand, her hand mere inches from Logan's gun.

"Let me say goodbye," Logan said thickly. He leaned forward over Ashley, pressing a kiss against her forehead, and closing the gap enough that her fingers brushed the cool metal of his gun.

"Back away!" Will barked. "Now."

Logan raised his hands, flinching at the pain in his still healing shoulder, and pulled away from Ashley. His eyes locked onto hers—one last, lingering look in case everything went terribly wrong. She'd only get one chance, because as soon as Will saw the gun, he'd shoot.

Her fingers latched onto the grip, pulling the gun out of Logan's holster at the same time he moved out of her line of sight. She didn't hesitate.

The gun fired, its near deafening crack followed by a shot from Will's gun. The recoil was more than Ashley's weak arm could handle and she dropped the weapon onto the hot sand, struggling to keep her head up to see what had happened.

Will was down. Her heart broke for him, but at the same time...she praised God that he was down.

But the second shot? Will's shot...?

"Logan?" she rasped, forcing her mouth to form his name. He was on the ground, a few feet away, and her throat constricted as she scanned the sand for blood. Not now, not after all of this. She couldn't lose him on a last, cheap shot. *"Logan?"*

But then he moved and the air rushed back into Ashley's lungs as he pushed up onto his hands and knees. The heavy weight in her ribs released as he crawled over to her and her chest heaved even though no tears could come.

"Shh." He cradled her head in his lap. "I'm here. His shot missed. You did it." His green eyes were full of emotion. So many things they'd left unsaid.

"Will?" she asked weakly.

"I'll check." Logan's voice was grim, his face clouded with sorrow. "And I'll call in our location on the radio. Stay with me, okay?"

She knew what he meant—here and now, because she was so weak—but her heart blurted out the answer.

"Always."

TWENTY

The whir of the helicopter rotors was the sweetest sound Logan had ever heard. He sat with his hands pressed against the bullet wound in Will's side, watching as the chopper set down a short distance away. It had been the longest minutes of his life, sitting ten feet away from Ashley as he tried to keep Will alive. He had kept talking to her, kept reassuring her, even though she was so weak she could barely move. If she had stopped responding... He was glad he hadn't had to make that choice to let Will bleed out.

"Thank You, Lord. They're here," he said almost as much to himself as to Ashley. She waved a limp hand.

He held that hand the entire way to the hospital in Alpine as the EMT hooked up an IV to her other arm and her eyes drifted shut from exhaustion. She looked peaceful now, and safe, and his heart overflowed with gratitude to God for letting him find her in time. And for protecting them from Will.

Will. The betrayal stung, especially when he remembered how close Sam and Will had been. How much had Will known about Sam's death? Had he been involved? There would be time to ask him those questions later. He, too, was hooked up to an IV, his body stable but unconscious for now. He would have a long road to recovery, only to awaken to a lifetime of consequences.

Ed Chambers met Logan in the ER waiting room a few hours later. "How is she?" He took a seat beside Logan.

"She'll be fine. The doc wants to keep her overnight to make sure."

"And Will?"

"In intensive care, but alive." He'd already told Ed everything that happened, and even though Jimenez wouldn't talk, they'd gotten one of his men to admit that Jimenez was Will Sykes's uncle.

Ed nodded. "Good work out there. I'm glad to see you all in one piece."

"She saved my life, you know." Logan ran a hand through his hair. The horror of that moment, when Will had pulled the gun on them, might stick with him for the rest of his life. He'd been so worried about Ashley, and so relieved at finding her, he'd barely even paid attention to Will.

"I know. You've told me a few times." Ed's eyes sparkled. "I guess we'll need to hire a couple of new law-enforcement rangers now. Especially after I retire in a few months and you take over as chief ranger."

Logan raised his brows. He knew Ed would have to retire eventually, but— "A few months? You never said anything about it before."

"I've been toying with the idea for a while. It's time."

"Barclay would never pick me as your replacement." Especially if he knew Logan had suspected him of working with Jimenez. But after Ed finished laughing at his suspicions, he'd vouched for the superintendent. Apparently the call he'd overheard had had something to do with Barclay's daughter in college.

"He will now." Ed laughed quietly. "I think you've proved yourself."

Ashley awoke to bright sunlight. She had to check the clock before she had any clue how long she'd slept. The entire night, apparently.

Beside her, Logan sat awkwardly crammed into a chair. His eyes were shut and his head lolled to one side. As she shifted in the bed, he stirred.

"Hey," he said groggily, rubbing his thumb and forefinger over his eyes. He straightened and looked her over from head to toe and back, his eyes pausing on the IV set in her left arm. "How are you feeling?"

"Like a rehydrated raisin." She grinned.

"At least you've gotten your sense of humor back." He grew silent, studying his hands. "We contacted the FBI. I spoke with your boss, let him know what happened and that you were okay."

"Thank you," she said, suddenly acutely aware of the space between them. That gap she'd almost forgotten, filled by the wedge that was Big Bend National Park and the Federal Bureau of Investigation. So strange they could both be in law enforcement yet still be worlds apart.

Logan reached out to her, enclosing her hand in his own. The warmth radiated through her whole body.

"How long have you been here?" she asked, torn between letting his hand go now to get it over with or clinging on for dear life.

"Since we brought you in." He grinned sheepishly. "There were probably other things I should've been doing, but...I had to make sure you were okay."

She squeezed his hand. "Thank you, Logan, for everything."

"Of course. I wish I could have done the same for Sam. At least now I know it wasn't his fault, or mine. It was Jimenez. And he'll have a lifetime in jail to answer for his crimes."

She almost didn't want to ask. "And Will?"

Logan stared down at their hands, intertwining his fingers with hers. "Alive and recovering. I don't think he can avoid jail time, but at least we've learned a little bit more about why he did it. One of Rico Jimenez's men told us everything he knew. Jimenez has been threatening Elena Sykes and her family for years, ever since he found them in El Paso. Apparently after Will's father refused to join the cartel, he died under mysterious circumstances. Then Jimenez pressured Will into joining by threatening his sister."

"That's awful." Despite everything, Ashley shivered. No one deserved to be put in that position. If only he had chosen a different path—asked for help.

"That was about three years ago," Logan went on, "right before Will applied for the job here, and right after Jimenez finally got his hands on that old map to the mine."

"I take it Will verified its existence once he worked here?"

"I'd assume so. Jimenez has been running drugs through the park on the side, but his main goal was to remove the gold. He chose summer because he knew there'd be less people out in the park to discover him."

It ought to have been awkward, sitting there, fingers interlaced, discussing a case, but Ashley couldn't imagine anything more natural. They had to talk about their relationship. She had to pull away. But not yet. "Where were they taking the gold?"

"Just as we thought—down past Mariscal Mountain and across the river." Logan paused, studying her. "What happened yesterday morning, Ashley? How did they get into your house?"

"Will came to my door and I let him in. Just to talk. And then it all came back to me, how I'd seen the drug deal and he'd thrown me into the river..." She couldn't help trembling at the memory. How she'd nearly panicked when she realized the truth. Taking a deep breath, she recounted everything for Logan. "And when I woke up, they'd taken me to Jimenez."

"Of course." Understanding dawned in his eyes. "But Will wasn't the one who drove off with you—that would have been too risky. So they sent another man to meet Will at your back window, and that's why there was no sign of forced entry. Or a struggle."

"No." She frowned. "I never had a chance."

"Smart on their part—" his lips tilted "—because I've seen what you can do."

Yes, he had. She smiled, too, despite it all. Then she wiggled her bandaged feet. "I never had a chance to put on my boots."

He raised an eyebrow, giving her a mock frown. "I noticed. I was thinking about firing you. Obviously you haven't been paying attention during training."

She laughed, but right behind the joy came a pang of grief. They'd talked about the case. There would be paperwork, suspects to question, reports to file. Maybe a trial. But they would still end up in two different cities, with two separate lives, and they hadn't had that conversation yet. Probably because thinking about it made her heart feel like it was being trampled by a bison.

She sighed, soul deep, and began to retract her fingers. Logan opened his hand, letting her pull back. "Don't."

Even in the hospital bed, covered by those starchy, thick, white sheets, she was beautiful. Letting her fingers slide away from his was the hardest thing Logan had ever done. It had to be her choice, but he couldn't give her up without at least telling her the truth. After all they'd been through, he owed it to her.

"Don't," he repeated, and her hand stopped, her fingers barely touching his. "Ashley, when I thought I'd lost you…when I thought you would die the way Sam had…" Water pooled in his eyes and he blinked it away. "I couldn't bear it that I'd never told you how I feel, how I care about you. I know we haven't known each other for long, and it doesn't make sense, but…I love you. More than I ever thought possible. It's like I've been missing something my whole life and…it's you."

There, he'd said it. Fragile heart held out for her to take or destroy. A great weight lifted off his chest, even though he had no idea how she'd respond. He knew she cared about him, but how much? Enough to find a way to be together?

Ashley's brown eyes went wide, her lips parting slightly. But when her hand slipped back into his, Logan's heart beat double time.

Her words were soft and he leaned closer to hear. "I thought I was going to die out there, the same way my brother did. But even being that close to the end, I never felt alone." Her voice hitched as she spoke and, after a brief pause, she continued, "I knew God was with me, and that no matter what, I'd spend eternity with Him. And I knew you were out there, searching for me, and that you wouldn't give up."

"We made a pretty good team, didn't we?" Her words hadn't exactly been what he'd wanted to hear, but he would still let her go. It might split his heart in two, but it had to be her choice. And he would still rejoice that she had found the path back to trusting the God he loved so much.

"Logan…" A tear slipped down her cheek and Logan's chest ached at what was coming. "I…" She sniffled as another tear broke loose.

"Shh," he said, unable to resist the urge to calm her, protect her, even from emotional pain. "It's okay, you don't have to say it. I understand." Or he would, someday. He hoped. He started to pull his hand away.

Ashley held on tightly. "No, that's not it." Her voice was muffled by the tears streaming down her cheeks. "I can't imagine life without you. I'm completely, madly in love with you, Ranger Logan Everett."

Logan couldn't contain the grin that broke out on his face. He wiped her cheek with his thumb. "But only people who don't like me use my last name."

"Except me." She smiled, blinking away the tears. "I love you, all of you, last name included."

Perhaps enough to make it her own one day? Logan didn't ask, but her eyes held the promise of the future.

She pulled her hand from his and reached up to lay it on his cheek. "Now, kiss me, please."

"Does that mean you're asking?" He leaned closer, until their faces were inches apart.

"Begging."

That was all he needed to hear.

EPILOGUE

Ashley stood by a window in the Chisos Lodge, staring out as puffy white clouds drifted high above the mountaintops. She couldn't have asked for a more spectacular day. It was April and the weather was gorgeous—past the rain and cold nights of winter, but not into the triple-digit temperatures of summer yet. Even after six months, she wasn't sure she'd ever become accustomed to the beauty of this place.

It probably should have been harder to leave her job as a federal agent and move to Big Bend. But after working here as a law-enforcement ranger, she could not imagine going back to Washington. Dick Barclay and Ed Chambers had been more than happy to give her the job. Special Agent in Charge Morton, while sad to lose her, had understood.

There was a noise behind her and Ashley turned to find a breathtakingly handsome man in a tuxedo enter the room.

"Logan Everett," she objected, "you're not supposed to see the bride before the wedding."

He paused, his gaze sweeping from the flowing hemline of her gown, past the simple, flattering neckline, to the pile of glossy brown curls on her head.

"I couldn't help it." He walked up to her and Ashley's heart raced at the nearness of him. "Ranger Thompson," he said breathlessly, "you are the most beautiful woman I've ever seen."

She smiled, taking in the love and admiration shining from his eyes. "You'll have to call me Ranger Everett soon."

"I can't imagine anything I'd like better. Maybe besides kissing you." He arched an eyebrow.

Her cheeks heated and she gave his arm a playful swat. "Don't you have somewhere else to be?"

"I'm going." He took a step back, but his eyes lingered. "Just wanted to make sure you were ready."

"I've never been more ready for anything in my life."

Logan's grin lit up his eyes. "Then let's get hitched, soon-to-be Ranger Everett."

And when Ashley stepped out into the bright Texas sunlight, her arm linked through her father's, and her heart full of God's goodness, she walked down the aisle toward Logan and the hope of a bright future before them.

* * * * *

If you enjoyed this book, pick up these other exciting stories from Love Inspired Suspense.

True Blue K-9 Unit Christmas
by Laura Scott and Maggie K. Black

Amish Christmas Hideaway
by Lenora Worth

Holiday Homecoming Secrets
by Lynette Eason

Christmas Witness Pursuit
by Lisa Harris

Silent Night Suspect
by Sharee Stover

Find more great reads at www.LoveInspired.com

Dear Reader,

Thank you for sharing Ashley and Logan's journey with me. We don't all experience the life-threatening situations they faced, but we do wrestle with our own pain, grief and loss. These things are an inevitable part of life in a fallen world. My prayer is that, like Ashley, you'll remember at those times how great God's love is for you. No matter how hard the circumstances, we never have to face them alone.

When I was in graduate school several years ago, I had the privilege of camping in Big Bend National Park. The majestic and rugged beauty of this remote and rarely visited place stuck with me, making it a natural choice for the setting of this novel. If you ever have the chance to visit, you will realize I've taken the liberty of rearranging park trails, altering the operations of the National Park Service, and reviving an old city across the border in Mexico. But hopefully you'll also find it to be as beautiful and awe-inspiring as I've attempted to portray.

I love hearing from readers, so please connect with me at www.kellievanhorn.com, where you can also learn more about my work.

Warm regards,
Kellie VanHorn

WE HOPE YOU ENJOYED THIS BOOK!

Love Inspired ®

SUSPENSE

Uncover the truth in these thrilling stories of faith in the face of crime from Love Inspired Suspense. Discover six new books available every month, wherever books are sold!

It couldn't be.

Ice filled Ashley Willis's veins despite the spring sunshine streaming through the living room windows of the Bristle Township home in Colorado where she rented a bedroom.

Disbelief cemented her feet to the floor, her gaze riveted to the horrific images on the television screen.

Flames shot out of the two-story building she'd hoped never to see again. Its once bright red awnings were now singed black and the magnificent stained glass windows depicting the image of an angry bull were no more.

She knew that place intimately.

The same place that haunted her nightmares.

The newscaster's words assaulted her. She grabbed on to the back of the faded floral couch for support.

"In a fiery inferno, the posh Burbank restaurant The Matador was consumed by a raging fire in the wee hours of the morning. Firefighters are working diligently to douse the flames. So far there have been no fatalities. However, there has been one critical injury."

Ashley's heart thumped painfully in her chest, reminding her to breathe. Concern for her friend Gregor, the man who had safely spirited her away from the Los Angeles area one frightening night a year and a half ago when she'd witnessed her boss, Maksim Sokolov, kill a man, thrummed through her. She had to know what happened. She had to know if Gregor was the one injured.

She had to know if this had anything to do with her.

"Mrs. Marsh," Ashley called out. "Would you mind if I use your cell phone?"

Her landlady, a widow in her mideighties, appeared in the archway between the living room and kitchen. Her hot-pink tracksuit hung on her stooped shoulders, but it was her bright smile that always tugged at Ashley's heart. The woman was a spitfire, with her blue-gray hair and her kind green eyes behind thick spectacles.

"Of course, dear. It's in my purse." She pointed to the black satchel on the dining room table. "Though you know, as I keep saying, you should get your own cell phone. It's not safe for a young lady to be walking around without any means of calling for help."

They had been over this ground before. Ashley didn't want anything attached to her name.

Or rather, her assumed identity—Jane Thompson.

Don't miss
Secret Mountain Hideout *by Terri Reed,*
available January 2020 wherever
Love Inspired Suspense books and ebooks are sold.

LoveInspired.com